PRODIGAL

A SCI-FI ALIEN WARRIOR ROMANCE

RAIDER WARLORDS OF THE VANDAR
BOOK SEVEN

TANA STONE

BROADMOOR BOOKS

CHAPTER
ONE

Ronnan

"Approaching Vandar territory, Raas."

I flinched at the words from my battle chief as I stood on the command deck and peered out the view screen. The blackness of space appeared just as vast and cold as it had during our entire long journey across the galaxy, but now the cold darkness was considered the realm of the Vandar. My lip curled at the thought.

I flicked a quick gaze across the warriors surrounding me. They stood at attention at their high consoles, their chests bare and marked with dark, curling marks etched across hard muscle. Leather battle kilts hung low around their waists and menacing, curved-blade battle axes were hooked onto metal-studded belts. My crew looked every bit the Vandar raiders who'd worn this ancient battle gear when they'd roamed the plains of the

1

home world in hordes before our planet had been devastated by the Zagrath and our people had been forced to take to the skies. The long tails twitching behind my warriors were the only things that betrayed the emotions we all felt about returning to a part of space that had once been our ancestors' and to a people we'd once called kin but did no longer.

I grunted roughly and swung my gaze back to the glass. We might be Vandar, but we did not belong to the Vandar who now ruled this space, and who'd defeated the Zagrath Empire. Not since we'd been exiled.

"But now we return for our birthright," I said, so low that my words were more like a murmured oath. "Vengeance."

I spun and stomped toward my *majak*, leaping to the raised level and making the steel floor rattle at the heavy impact of my boots. My first officer's arms were braced on his hips as he surveyed the command crew, and he nodded at me as I took my place by his side.

"Is it as you expected, Ayden?" I asked my oldest friend without turning my head to look at him.

He was silent for a beat then one shoulder jerked almost reflexively. "It looks just like home, but it feels nothing like our far corner of the galaxy."

I understood his words. The blackness of space might look alike, but knowing we were in territory that no one in our horde had laid eyes on before made my stomach churn. It had been our fathers who had revolted against the Vandar leaders and been defeated. They had been cast out to live the rest of their lives in unknown space, take alien mates, and survive without the protection of the hordes. They'd called themselves the Kyrie Vandar—the Lost Vandar—but it was our generation who'd been raised with a hunger for revenge so powerful it had compelled us to return.

"We will do what our fathers could not," I told my *majak*. "We will claim our rightful place among the Vandar hordes."

He cut his eyes to me. "If we can find them. The warriors and rebels we've encountered have only *heard* of the Vandar. They did not know how we could track them."

I frowned. The Vandar might have defeated the Zagrath, but that didn't mean that they'd abandoned their desire to be unseen. We'd grown up hearing tales of the raiding warlords who flew invisibly, their hordes of cruel warbirds emerging like dark wraiths to surprise their enemy. When our fathers had rebuilt their own hordes, they had followed in the footsteps of those they'd turned against and even now, we moved through the skies invisibly.

"Even in the far reaches of the galaxy the tales of the Vandar victory have spread. Would valiant heroes remain hidden now that the enemy has been destroyed?"

Ayden cocked his head. "If they do, we will find them."

I growled my agreement. Word had reached us that the three brothers who'd led the victory—three warlords of their own hordes—were sons of Raas Bardon, the notorious Raas who had defeated my own father and Ayden's so many moons ago. They were the ones I sought. The old Raas might have passed on to Zedna, but his sons would pay the price he never did.

"And when we do find them, Ronnan?" My friend asked, dropping his voice so that the rest of the crew didn't hear him address me by my name on the command deck.

I didn't mind him dropping my title. Ayden knew me better than anyone alive and had grown up by my side. It was only because I was more ruthless and he more cunning that I was Raas, and he was my first officer. But the truth was that we led and ruled our horde together, and I relied on his counsel as much as I relied on the iron sky ship that now flew me to my destiny.

"We will demand to be given a place of honor that was denied our fathers." I curled my hands into fists by my side. "Or they will regret that the Kyrie Vandar ever returned."

"I suspect they will regret that in any case," Ayden laughed grimly. "If Bardon's sons are anything like their father, they will not welcome a challenge."

"We do not have to be a challenge." I slid one hand to the hilt of my battle axe, the cool metal steadying my drumming heart. "We bring many warbirds and many warriors to add to the Vandar might."

My *majak* folded his arms across his chest. "But we are not like them. Not anymore."

I glanced at the broad-shouldered warrior at my side, his platinum hair falling down his shoulders. We both had the coloring of our Selkee mothers, as did most of our crew, which put us in stark contrast to the black hair of the typical Vandar. But the Selkee had welcomed our exiled fathers when they'd been bedraggled and wandering through space, sharing the bounty of their planet as well as their beautiful females, who had become mates to the Kyrie Vandar.

"If the rumors are true, the Vandar do not care so much about pure blood anymore," I reminded him. Along with word of the

Vandar defeat of the Zagrath, the whispers were that the Raases had taken human brides.

I flicked my fingers through my pale hair, wondering for a beat if the Vandar would even recognize us as members of their species since we were the result of intermingling with aliens not even found in this sector. Then I bristled at the thought of being rejected because of my mother's blood. My mother had been the only one to shield me and my brother from my father's often brutal temper, and she held the only soft spot in my heart. I would die to protect her honor, and I would strike down anyone who dared insult her.

Ayden rocked back on his heels. "Then perhaps this will be a reunion and not a challenge to the terms of the exile."

I didn't respond. I couldn't allow myself to hope for anything but the battle I knew we were provoking by returning after so many moons. Even if the old Vandar who'd cast out our fathers were long gone, there was a score to settle with those who'd inherited their power. Someone had to pay for the wrongs inflicted on the Kyrie Vandar. "It will be the reckoning that the Vandar deserve."

"Picking up a vessel, Raas." My battle chief's voice boomed, echoing off the exposed metal of the command deck.

"A Vandar warbird?" My fingers tingled in anticipation, although I was surprised one of our vessels would be so easy to locate.

Kaiven scowled at the console and straightened, the leather and iron body armor that crisscrossed his chest rattling. "No, Raas."

Tvek. I knew it couldn't be so easy.

"Zagrath?" My heart raced at the thought of finding an enemy vessel the Vandar might have missed. It would feel good to destroy the enemy, even if it wasn't the enemy that had haunted my thoughts for longer than I could remember.

My battle chief braced his hands on either side of the console and shook his head, his hair swinging around his face. "It doesn't carry a Zagrath signature. It's also powered down."

I grunted. This discovery was turning out to be a disappointment. "A mystery ship floating in space? On screen."

The wide view of scattered stars vanished, and the glass that stretched across the front of the command deck was taken up with the image of a ship that didn't look much larger than a transport. It also looked as if it had been in one too many space battles, with scorch marks and dents marring its silver hull. There was no identifying insignia on the side. Not that I would have known the symbols for the factions in this sector if there were any left.

"Life signs?" I asked.

Kaiven tilted his head and then swiveled it to me. "One, Raas. A female."

A female, alone on a ship that wasn't moving? My pulse quickened. Things had gotten interesting.

CHAPTER
TWO

Sloane

"Shitballs!" I slammed my palm against the console in my cockpit. Why had I insisted on taking out the oldest ship in the Valox resistance fleet?

"Because you're a stubborn pain in the ass, and you refuse to believe that the Zagrath are really gone," I muttered to myself, as I tried to get the engine to start again, and the sounds of vintage Earth rock music played in my earpiece.

I was only repeating what I was sure others in the underground resistance had been saying since the Vandar had defeated the Zagrath. It wasn't that I didn't want to believe the empire was destroyed, but after spending half my life fighting them, I had a hard time believing it. Not when the Zagrath had controlled so many sectors and ruled so many planets. That kind of power didn't disappear overnight. No, that kind of evil festered in a dark place until it could resurface when you were least expecting it.

I hadn't been able to explain the gnawing feeling in my gut that they were still out there, but I also hadn't been able to ignore it. I'd always operated on a heavy dose of gut instinct—and it had served me well as a pilot—and now was no different. Maybe it was so many little things—the lack of any Zagrath ships on their abandoned outposts, the enemy prisoners who stayed defiant in the face of prison, the fact that the number of Zagrath ships destroyed didn't come close to matching our initial estimates of their fleet—that had convinced me that our enemy was not gone for good.

I huffed out a breath. Too bad I was the only pilot in the resistance that believed the Zagrath were only dormant and not destroyed. They might have been severely weakened by the Vandar attacks, but I was convinced some of them had slunk off to hide.

"And I'm going to find them." I frowned at my readouts and tapped at my earpiece to stop the music. "If I can get this hunk of junk to move again."

I leaned back in the pilot's seat and gazed out onto the vastness of space. Okay, so coming out to the edge of the sector might not have been the best idea, especially not alone. But none of my fellow resistance fighters had wanted to come with me again. After joining me on my search for nearly a full standard lunar cycle and finding nothing, they'd lost their enthusiasm.

More like they'd decided to stop humoring me, I thought. Even Cassie and Thea, my best friends in the Valor resistance and the women I'd been working with since we'd gone through training together, had begged off for this mission.

I hated thinking that maybe they'd been right, and I needed to let it go and enjoy life without having to be on the run from the empire. But what was my life's purpose, if there was no empire to rebel against? I'd joined the freedom fighters as soon as I was old enough, and since that day, my life had been about fighting against the empire. I didn't know if I knew how to exist without having something to fight against.

"Come on, Sloane," I scolded myself. "This is what you've been fighting for. The former Zagrath colonies are free. The planets that were under their rule are free. We won!"

I sighed, my heart twisting in my chest as I thought of all the freedom fighters who hadn't survived to see the empire go down including Leo. The dull ache in my chest sharpened as I thought about the handsome, dark-skinned pilot. I'd known better than to fall for a fellow fighter, but it hadn't been a conscious choice. I'd fallen in love with him slowly, slipping a little more each time he'd winked at me or given me a conspiratorial grin. Before I knew it, when we weren't flying, we'd been inseparable. I'd even allowed myself to think of life with him after the Valox. Then he'd been shot down during an attack on a Zagrath freighter, and all my dreams had morphed into a need to avenge him. A need that hadn't faded when the empire had been defeated.

I thought of the Valox resistance slowly disbanding and fighters returning to their home worlds. What had seemed like a tight-knit family as we'd fought side by side against the empire was now unraveling, and I was spinning—unmoored and alone—through the universe. It felt like the furthest thing from winning.

I gave my head a firm shake and returned my focus to the cockpit. "What feels even less like winning is being stranded in space."

All I had to do was send out a distress call and the Valor would come get me, but I'd yet to swallow my pride and send the transmission. I dreaded the looks I'd get when I arrived in a clunker ship that had to be towed in after finding no trace of the Zagrath I was convinced were out there. At least I didn't need to worry anymore about being ambushed by imperial patrols. Even a skeptic like me had to admit there were a lot of benefits to the Zagrath being defeated.

I glanced at the blinking red lights in the cockpit before standing. "I can fix this."

I wasn't a skilled engineer like Thea, but I knew the basics. I grimaced. At least, I had when I first started flying. It had been a while since I'd needed to analyze my ship's engine.

"Doesn't matter." I strode to the center of the compact ship as I tugged my frizzy brown hair into an even tighter ponytail and turned on my music again. "I don't have a choice. I either fix this thing so I can fly back to base, or I get towed back with my tail between my legs."

I yanked up the center hatch and clambered down to where I could access the engine. Standing surrounded by flashing lights and circuit boards, I scrunched my mouth to one side as the thumping beat of the music helped me focus. Okay, maybe it had been longer than I'd remembered since I'd had to fiddle with the mechanics of a ship.

"Come on, Sloane. You can do this." I tapped one foot on the steel grate beneath me and the sound echoed over my music. "All you have to do is channel your inner Thea."

I almost laughed out loud at this. Thea was always cool under pressure and completely unflappable. She didn't believe in anything she couldn't see or prove, and she definitely didn't think the Zagrath were still lurking in the shadows. If there was a person who was my polar opposite, it was my friend Thea. And if there was anyone I needed right at this moment, it was her. Cassie would have joined me in freaking out, but Thea would have quietly gotten to work and fixed the problem, while the rest of us were bracing for the worst.

I squared my shoulders and squinted at the complex innards of the vessel, determined to figure out what was wrong. I bopped my head along with the vintage song, wondering briefly what it meant to smell like teen spirit before forcing myself to talk out the problem. "If propulsion is gone and the engines have lost power, that means the problem is in the—"

The ship jolted to one side, and I stumbled into a circuit board. "Son of a Grednar!"

Glancing around, I saw that the engines hadn't restarted, so why had the ship jerked? I rubbed my aching shoulder and hoisted myself to the center of the ship. There was no way the resistance had already sent a rescue ship to tractor me back. I hadn't been gone long enough to be missed.

I made my way to the cockpit, cursing to myself, but when I reached the compact area with its view into space, there was nothing. Had I imagined the ship moving? I touched a hand to my shoulder, which still twinged from the impact against the steel circuit board. Nope. The bruise I would no doubt get was no hallucination.

"Must have been space debris." I scanned the sky again, grateful that whatever had hit me hadn't been larger. Usually, my sensors would have alerted me to incoming objects, but I guessed those were on the fritz, too.

No engines. No sensors. I groaned. It was time to admit that I was stuck and to call for help. I'd never hear the end of it from the rest of the resistance—what was left of them—but I didn't have much choice.

"First thing when I get back, I'm having Thea give me a refresher in mechanics." I sank into the pilot's seat and reached for the communications console. Even without power, I could activate a distress call.

The ship shuddered again, and a shiver of fear slid down my spine. That hadn't been space debris. Even over my music, I heard sounds behind me. Sounds that weren't the result of a glitchy ship or wayward space rocks.

I popped out my earpiece and turned around, my heart lurching in my chest when I saw two enormous males blocking the entrance to the cockpit, their broad chests crisscrossed with leather straps, and their tails swishing behind them. Then my shoulder muscles uncoiled as I recognized the battle kilts that revealed muscular thighs and the black ink curling across their chests and shoulders.

I'd been found by the Vandar!

Then I noticed that their hair wasn't black, like it was on every other Vandar I'd seen. It was platinum. And they held their gleaming battle axes as if they were ready to attack.

Shitballs.

CHAPTER
THREE

Ronnan

My pulse surged as we locked onto the small ship and forced its hatch open. It had been a long time since I'd personally joined a raiding party, although boarding this insignificant ship hardly seemed to qualify. Still, it was a vessel in Vandar territory, which made it our concern.

"Our property," I growled under my breath, reminding myself that the Vandar claimed any ship that ventured into its space. Since we were Vandar, that meant that this ship, and anything in it, now belonged to us.

Raiding had been the Vandar way of life after our people had been forced from our destroyed home world by the Zagrath. We'd had the choice to live under their rule or become outlaws. There had been no choice. The Vandar would never submit to anyone or be controlled by a cruel empire. We'd taken to the skies, secreting our women and children in hidden colonies, while our warriors had swarmed space in flying hordes to terrorize the Zagrath and all who were loyal to them.

Even in exile, the Kyrie Vandar had continued the Vandar tradition of hordes and raiding, although we'd become more pirates than rebels. Without an empire to fight, our hordes had sharpened our skills by raiding syndicate ships and redistributing their bounty to impoverished planets.

"No resistance, Raas." Kaiven stepped onto the ship with his battle axe in front of him. He swung his head from side to side. "No sign of the single occupant."

I grunted, trying not to let my disappointment engulf me. I should not have expected to encounter a Vandar warbird so easily. They were Vandar, after all.

My battle chief strode forward, along with one of his warriors, the flaps of their battle kilts slapping their legs as they strode toward the nose of the ship. I followed behind, my hand resting on the hilt of my axe and my fingers drumming to the beat of our heavy footsteps.

The ship's interior was much like the exterior—battered and old, the dingy metal showing signs of wear. At least it wasn't a pleasure cruiser or a passenger vessel. The utilitarian design and weapons strapped to the walls told me that it was a fighting ship, which made my heart beat faster.

Then I frowned. What was a single female doing in a war ship? As far as I knew, the Zagrath didn't send their females into battle. If this wasn't a Vandar ship and we hadn't boarded a Zagrath vessel, what had we taken? Was there a new enemy encroaching on Vandar territory?

Kaiven had come to a stop in front of me, his broad body and that of the other warrior blocking the narrow entrance to the ship's cockpit. I made a low noise in my throat, and they parted enough to let me step inside.

If I'd been hoping to find an impressively armed fighter, or even a bulky, alien female like the husky ones on Parven Prime who were virtually indistinguishable from the males until they shed their body armor, I would have been disappointed. The creature who stood quickly from the pilot's seat barely reached my shoulder and didn't wear armor or brandish weapons. She was dressed in a snug, black, flight suit and had brown hair pulled up high that puffed out like a frizzy tail behind her head. Her dark eyes were wide, and her skin tan. She had no tail, no horns, and no visible markings.

"What are you?" I asked, making no effort to hide my gaze that roamed up and down her body.

"What am I?" Her voice cracked before she straightened her shoulders. "I'm a pilot with the Valox resistance."

Valox resistance? I'd never heard of this, but if these fighters sent out such slight females they couldn't be much of a threat. "Are all Valox as small as you?"

A line formed between her eyes as she looked at me. "Valox isn't a species. I'm human. The Valox resistance is made up of lots of species, but shouldn't you know this?"

I ignored her question. She was human. The species was not unknown to me, but I hadn't been aware they were warriors. "Do you work for the empire?"

She jerked back as if I'd slapped her, her brow furrowing. "Are you fucking kidding me? The Valox are freedom fighters who've been working against the empire forever." She tilted her head at me. "Wait. You're Vandar, aren't you?"

"We are Vandar." There was no need to tell her that we were the lost Vandar back to seek revenge and restitution. Not yet. "I am Raas Ronnan."

"I'm Sloane." The female smiled at me. "And we're allies. We worked together to bring down the Zagrath, right?"

I gave a curt nod. "But this is Vandar territory, is it not?"

"Technically, but now that the entire sector is free from the empire, all those old boundaries are meaningless."

I stepped closer to her. "Are they?"

She gulped and nodded, trying to back up but only bumping against her console. "The Vandar don't need to raid anymore since the empire has been," she paused for a beat, "destroyed."

Behind me, Kaiven grunted his disapproval, but I didn't turn. I kept my gaze locked on the female, whose pupils had flared wider. It had been even longer than we'd raided a ship that I'd encountered a female who wasn't claimed by another or given coin to feign desire.

"The raiders of the Vandar no longer raid?" I darted a hand quickly to capture her chin and tilt it up so that she was forced to meet my gaze. "Is this true?"

She sucked in a fast breath, nodding. "Of course. Why would I lie?"

"Maybe you're a spy for the empire," I suggested, studying her face for any signs of deception.

Her eyes narrowed in obvious anger and disgust. "I'd die before I'd work for the empire."

The heat that flashed in her eyes made me believe her. She despised the Zagrath. I slid my hand down to her neck, feeling the quick pulse beneath her jaw and the unexpected arrow of desire that shot through me.

I scowled and tightened my grip. Did this tailless female arouse me? She was nothing like Vandar females or even the perfumed pleasurers who painted their faces and draped themselves in sumptuous fabrics, but there was something about the challenge in her eyes that made my cock twitch and my heart hammer in my chest. My gaze slid from her eyes to her mouth, the curve of her pink lips begging me to taste them.

Kaiven cleared his throat, and I loosened my grip on the female, released her, and stepped back.

"Who are you?" she asked, her eyes flitting to my hair. "Are you really Vandar?"

Rage tangled with desire, both sending heat swirling through my veins in a stormy torrent. There should be no doubt that we were Vandar, and if she had been a male, I would have proven it to her by lopping off her head. But her head was far too pretty. "We *are* Vandar, and you should be more frightened of us than you are, female."

She folded her arms across her chest. "If you're Vandar, then you know that we're on the same side. I have no reason to be afraid of you."

If any other warrior had challenged me in such a way, I would have struck him down with my axe in a single swipe, but this creature was not like any other warrior. I eyed her carefully, my fingers tingling with the desire to tear her clothes from her body and show her exactly why she should fear me, but I steadied my temper and my pounding arousal.

If what she said was true, then she might have more than one use for me. An ally of the Vandar would know where they were or at least how to find them. If the Vandar valued these Valox as allies, then they might be motivated to save this female.

I turned on my heel. "*Vaes!*" I strode forward then paused and glanced over my shoulder to where the female stood unmoving. "Come."

"Come? With you?"

I blew out an impatient breath. "Yes. You will come with me."

She shook her head. "I don't think so." She pivoted and reached across her console. "I'd rather send out a distress call and wait to be towed back."

I lunged for her so quickly that she screamed when I spun her, coiled an arm around her waist, and jerked her flush to me. "That was not a request. It was a command, and I suggest you obey it, just as I suggest you obey all my commands in the future."

She struggled to free herself from my grasp. "What the fuck? You can't do this to me. The Vandar and Valox are allies. You can't just take me from my ship."

I leaned down so that my lips brushed her ear, as I ran the tip of my tail up the inside of one of her legs. "We aren't *those* Vandar, and I assure you I can do anything I want with you."

CHAPTER
FOUR

Sloane

I jerked away from the Raas, but the tail which had curled tightly around my legs prevented me from running. The buzz of his words had sent undesired tremors down my spine, and I fought the shivers that threatened to wrack my body.

He straightened to his full height, towering over me as he held my gaze silently before turning and motioning with his head to one of his raiders. "Bring her."

I knew it was pointless to fight them since they were massive and armed, and I'd stupidly left my blaster hanging on the wall. Even if I could reach it, there was no way I could take out all of them before they brought me down.

I glanced at the glinting, curved edge of the battle axe and swallowed hard. I did not want to be on the receiving end of that.

Still, I couldn't stop myself from resisting as the two Vandar each grabbed one of my arms and propelled me from the cockpit and through the ship. My feet barely touched the floor as I was practically dragged along, and I finally stopping struggling once we reached the place where their ship was latched onto mine.

How had I not heard their ship lock on and pry open my hatch? I thought of the tiny earbuds in my pocket and sighed. Cassie always said that my obsession with old Earth rock would be my downfall one day, but I'd always thought that was because she couldn't stand hearing the stuff. Not that I could have done much even if I had heard the Vandar coming, but at least I could have gotten off a distress call. Now the Valox wouldn't have any idea what had happened to me.

My gut twisted as I thought of my best friends and what they'd think when I didn't return. Would they come searching for me? Would they even know where to look?

The two hulking warriors pushed me into their vessel where the Raas stood waiting for me with one hand gripping a high, metal bar running along the ceiling. There were no seats, but before I could ask where I should go, the rest of the Vandar piled in and crowded around me, all of them holding the bar overhead.

I suppressed the urge to make a dash for it before the ship disengaged from mine, but then the hatch slammed shut and the steel floor rumbled beneath my feet. Raas Ronnan curled an arm around my waist and his tail wrapped around my legs as the ship blasted off, and I swayed from the sudden movement and bumped against his bare chest.

I raised my hands to brace myself, splaying them on his hard, ridged stomach and feeling him inhale sharply. I was enveloped by hulking, Vandar raiders, their bodies swaying along with mine, but it was the Raas whose heat radiated into me. I tried to pull my hands away, but the ship tilted and sent me into him hard, and he tightened his grip to hold me to him.

"There is no point in fighting it," he said, his voice a low hum that matched the rumble of the engines.

I didn't know if he meant the motion of the ship or something more, but I didn't like it either way. But he was right. Since I wasn't tall enough to reach the overhead bar they all held, the only way I wouldn't pinball around was if he held me steady.

I felt the eyes of all the Vandar on me, as we flew with their warlord holding me. All except for the Raas. He wasn't looking at me, but his entire body was tense, except for the tip of his tail, which was vibrating against my leg.

It's fine, I told myself as I tried to calm my breathing. This is all a big misunderstanding. Maybe this horde hadn't fought with the Valox resistance and didn't understand our alliance. After all, the defeat of the Zagrath had spanned across multiple sectors and the imperial control was still being dismantled. I wasn't sure how many Vandar hordes there were, but it made sense that not all of them were involved in the main battles.

What was not fine was the way this Raas was affecting me. My fingers prickled from touching his bare skin, and my heart pounded as if I'd just pulled off a combat landing after executing a dozen barrel rolls. I hadn't reacted this way since Leo, and even he hadn't provoked such a violent reaction. I hoped it was the fear making my hands tremble. If it wasn't, I was in more trouble than I wanted to admit.

Before I could let my mind spiral, the ship shuddered hard as we landed. I released a breath as the Raas dropped his arm from overhead and the other Vandar followed suit. As the hatch opened, I expected him to unwind his tail and arm from me, but instead he rested his free hand on my hip for a moment as the rest of the warriors strode from the ship.

I tipped my head back to see that he was staring at me with his brow furrowed. My breath hitched in my throat but then he peered over my head.

"Take her to the *oblek*."

I opened my mouth to complain, or maybe beg—what was the *oblek*?—but I was pulled away and ushered quickly from the ship and into a massive space that had me forgetting all about the Raas and the *oblek*.

The Vandar transport had been utilitarian and compact, but the hangar bay we'd landed inside was anything but small. The ceiling soared above me, revealing what seemed to be the interior of a massive vessel that was a dimly lit labyrinth of criss-crossing metal bridges, coiling staircases, and suspended platforms. Shouts and thudding footfall echoed around me as my eyes adjusted to the shadows.

The two Vandar who'd dragged me earlier did the honors again, but this time I didn't bother to struggle. Where was I supposed to run anyway? I was on a Vandar warbird, and a big part of me was fascinated to actually see the interior of one of the mysterious horde ships. We might be allied with the Vandar, but that didn't mean they'd given us guided tours of their warbirds. Their massive, cloaked ships were still something few others had seen, and I couldn't stop myself from gaping as I was hurried up a series of staircases and suspended walkways that swayed as we crossed them.

If I'd been great with orienting myself like Cassie, I would have been trying to memorize the route, but that was why she was the navigator. I was crap with directions, and after the third winding staircase that went up, and the second that took us down again, I had no idea where I was.

When we reached an arched doorway that was as dark as the rest of the surfaces on the vessel, one of the Vandar flicked a hand to one side and it slid open.

"Leave us," he told the other Vandar.

The warrior bowed his head quickly. "Yes, Kaiven."

I was led inside to a room that was nearly pitch black. The only light came from a faint, blue glow in the recessed ceiling and the distant, flickering stars outside the wall of glass overlooking space. It only took my eyes a moment to adjust to this darker space, and I quickly noted the weapons strapped to the walls and the chains hanging from the ceiling. My stomach dropped. Now I knew *oblek* didn't mean hospitality suite.

The Vandar approached me quickly, patting me down so efficiently and brusquely that I didn't have time to squawk my complaints when he plucked the earbuds from my pocket. Not that I had anything to synch them with, I thought, and I decided not to lodge a complaint.

"I think you've got the wrong idea about me," I said once the Vandar had stepped back. "I'm not your enemy."

"Maybe not," the Raas said, as he entered from another door. "But you know how we can find our enemy."

Before the wide door swished shut behind him, I could see that it was the ship's bridge, complete with curious Vandar all wearing the same leather kilts, with axes hanging from their waists, and shocked expressions etched on their faces.

"You mean the Zagrath?" My pulse fluttered with excitement. Did the Vandar believe as I did that the empire wasn't really decimated?

The Raas took long, brisk steps until he was looming over me. "I mean the Vandar."

I leaned back but didn't cower. "How can the Vandar be your enemy when you're all Vandar, and you're flying in what's clearly a Vandar ship?"

"We are not the Vandar you know. We are the Kyrie Vandar— the Lost Vandar—that were exiled before either of us were born." His eyes scoured my face as he cupped my chin in one palm. "We've returned to exact our revenge and take what was stolen from us."

I shook my head, as much from confusion as anything else. Lost Vandar? Exiled Vandar?

He dragged the callused pad of his thumb roughly over my bottom lip. "And you're going to help us do it."

CHAPTER
FIVE

Ronnan

Confusion flickered behind her eyes as she tried to snatch her face from my grasp. "You aren't the Vandar who fought with the Valox to defeat the empire? You were exiled by the Vandar?"

I allowed a growl to escape from my throat as I released her, instantly missing the soft touch and warmth of her skin. "Not I." I gestured to the door that led to my command deck. "None of my horde were the ones exiled by the Vandar, but we have paid the price."

She took a step back, her gaze swiveling around the room that contained no furniture, only weapons lashed to the dark walls and straps and chains to restrain those who needed to be interrogated. "I don't understand. You look like the Vandar. Even your ship is exactly like everyone describes Vandar warbirds."

I eyed her, my tail vibrating behind me as if willing me to pounce on her. It would be so easy to tie her to the wall or string her up from the ceiling. Then she wouldn't dare question a Raas of the Vandar. Then she would fear me, as so many had when they'd been brought to my battle chief's *oblek*.

But I found that I didn't want her to fear me. Not in that way, although the desire to subdue her rebellious mouth and tame her inclination to challenge me pounded through me like the fiery rush of blood through my veins.

She was still an ally of the Vandar, I reminded myself as I pivoted from her and strode toward the wall of glass. She was a valuable source of information and a useful hostage. My own carnal desires were of no importance, and I forced the traitorous thoughts from my mind.

I did not desire such a small, helpless human female. The idea was absurd. I was a Raas of the Vandar. If and when I took a Raisa, she would need to be as valiant and powerful as I was. One of the reasons my horde had crossed the galaxy and violated the terms of our exile—aside from our unquenched thirst for revenge—was our need to find worthy mates.

Our sires had mated with the Selkee, but to restore our bloodlines to Vandar greatness, we required Vandar mates. Even as I thought this, I flinched at the implied betrayal of my own beloved mother. I would trade none of what I'd inherited from her—not even my distinctive platinum hair—but my father's words had been drilled into me for so long they felt as if they were my own. The purity and strength of the Vandar must be restored with Vandar mates.

"We are Vandar." I stared out at the black curtain of space. "Our fathers rebelled against the Vandar warlords and lost, which earned them exile from Vandar space and the hordes. They were cast out with only a single, aged warbird, and the axes on their backs. They settled on a distant planet, took non-Vandar mates, and built warbirds. They didn't live to see the hordes take to the skies and set a course for Vandar space, but it was their wish that we would return and claim what was taken from them."

"What was taken from you? You seem to have done pretty well for yourself if you created hordes from nothing."

I clasped my hands behind my back, squeezing hard. "We were branded as traitors and sent from the Vandar brotherhood. Our fathers were separated from their families and from intended mates. We were never spoken of again in the Vandar world. We were erased." I whirled around. "You have never heard of us. No one in this galaxy knows of our existence. Maybe not even the Raases who fought by your side. But they will know now."

The female shifted from one foot to the next. "I get why you'd be pissed, but I don't get what any of this has to do with me."

"You said you were an ally of the Vandar."

She sighed. "Well, yeah, but—"

I advanced on her. "Did you lie?"

"No." She shook her head quickly. "I told you the truth. I'm a pilot with the Valox resistance, and we fought with the Vandar to liberate the galaxy from the empire. All of that is true, but that doesn't mean I'm tight with the Vandar. It's not like I hang out on a regular basis with Raas Kratos or Raas Kaalek."

The hairs on the back of my neck pricked. "Kratos and Kaalek. Those are two of the three Raas brothers, the sons of the notorious Raas Bardon, aren't they?"

She shrugged. "I know they're brothers, but I don't know anything about their father. The Vandar lived in almost total secrecy until we banded together against the empire. Until that point, the entire galaxy believed they were terrorists, and the empire was the victim of their unprovoked raids. No one laid eyes on the Vandar and lived to tell about it."

I made a rough, approving sound in my throat. That was what my father had always told me about the Vandar. That they'd been considered outlaws, even though they were fighting against a tyrannical empire that kept every planet under its control impoverished and dependent. He'd related with pride how the Vandar had started raiding imperial ships to disrupt their control and had gained the reputation as vicious and cruel, even though they avoided civilian targets. Despite my need to exact revenge, I could not suppress the swell of pride in my chest at the thought of what the Vandar had done. Then that pride was doused by the sharp reminder of the brother I'd left behind.

I forced myself to think about anything but my fractured family as I folded my arms and peered down at the human. "Despite your claims, it sounds like you know a great deal about the Vandar."

"Mostly legend, although since the warlords took human brides, they haven't been as shy about being seen."

I'd heard the rumors about the females the Vandar had claimed as their Raisas, but a part of me found it incredulous. Frail, human females serving as Raisas of Vandar hordes? "You've seen these human brides?"

She raised an eyebrow at me. "One of them. Tara was pretty involved in the battles to take down the empire."

"She was a warrior?" I couldn't imagine a creature as small as this one being much of a threat to anyone.

The female before me put her hands on her hips. "You don't think human women can kick ass? I'll have you know I've blown more imperial fighters from the sky than almost any other Valox pilot."

The thought of her shooting down enemy ships made my cock thicken, but I only scowled. She was still a human, and I was not like the Raases who'd fallen prey to their charms. I'd returned to restore the honor and bloodline of the Kyrie Vandar, not muddle it further.

Still, her flashing eyes and heaving chest sent fresh pulses of hunger through me. There was no harm in enjoying the forbidden fruit, or in seeing what the other Vandar found so appealing. Taking a female to my bed didn't mean I would take her as a mate. I'd spent enough sweaty nights with pleasurers to understand that very well.

"If it's true that you're a valiant warrior, maybe I should add you to my crew."

She opened and closed her mouth. "I thought the Vandar didn't have females in their hordes. I thought your warbirds were sausage fests."

As soon as the words left her, she slapped a hand over her mouth. We did not have the word sausage in the Vandar tongue, but I knew what it was from my travels across the galaxy. It took me a beat to decipher her meaning and another moment to feel my lips twitch up as her cheeks flushed.

I stepped closer to her. "I am willing to make an exception, especially since I still believe you will be valuable to us when we find the Vandar."

She looked at me and blinked rapidly. "You're going to let me join your horde?"

I gave her the briefest of smiles before turning on my heel and heading for the door to the command deck. "No, I'm going to let you join me in my bed."

"What?" she spluttered behind me as I opened the door.

Kaiven stood on the other side, awaiting his own chance to interrogate the prisoner. "Your orders, Raas?"

"Take her to my quarters, Kaiven" I told him, my pulse tripping at the thought of continuing our dialogue with her wearing considerably less clothing. "And lock her in."

CHAPTER
SIX

Sloane

The warrior the Raas had called Kaiven stood to one side as the arched steel doors slid apart. We'd wound our way from the top of the warbird through more of the ship's suspended bridges that swayed from side to side as the vessel flew, until we'd reached the imposing entrance that had unfamiliar symbols etched at the top.

"You will remain here."

I peered into the space, which was as dimly lit and spartan as the rest of the ship. It didn't look any warmer in there than it was in the rest of the cold, cavernous vessel. When I saw an enormous bed at the far end with a headboard that appeared to have been forged from battle-axes, a shiver went through me. "You don't have a brig?"

The Vandar twisted his head to me, his pale hair falling forward. "You would rather stay in a cell than with our Raas?"

I thought back to the dominant glint in Raas Ronnan's eyes and nodded. "If I'm to be your prisoner, then I should be in the brig."

Kaiven grunted and braced his legs wide. "You are the guest of Raas Ronnan, and he has ordered that you stay here. And we have no brig." He raised one eyebrow. "Vandar take no prisoners."

It was pointless for me to stand in the corridor arguing with the guy. He had his orders, and it was clear he was going to carry out his directives. I darted a glance around me, as hulking Vandar leapt from one suspended platform to another and took steep staircases two steps at a time as they moved through the ship, their heavy boots thudding and making the metal rattle and clang.

Even if I did try to run, where would I go? The place was a maze designed for enormous Vandar. Not only did I not have any idea where things were, I was afraid one wrong step would send me plummeting down the cavernous open core.

"Fine," I grumbled and stepped into the Raas' quarters. Before I could turn and ask how long I would be stuck there, the doors behind me slid shut, leaving only a seam between the gunmetal-gray sides of the arch to give any clue that it was a doorway. I put my fingers to it and was startled by how tightly the cold metal was fused. I couldn't even wedge my fingernails between the two sides, much less pull them apart.

I scowled at the door but decided not to waste more time on it. It was as solid and unyielding as every other part of the Vandar vessel. I wouldn't be prying it open anytime soon.

I spun around and assessed the rest of the space. So, this was where Raas Ronnan lived? I wasn't sure if all Vandar ships looked the same in every respect, or if each Raas customized his quarters, but the dark furnishings and sleek surfaces fit the alien I'd encountered.

The floors were black and glossy, echoing as I walked across to the circular bed that was raised from the rest of the room. I had to tip my head back to take in the height of the menacing headboard, which touched the ceiling. The same symbols that had been etched over the doorway outside were carved into a curve of steel at the very top, and I wondered if it was Raas Ronnan's name in Vandar.

The bed itself was neatly covered in dove gray fabric that looked surprisingly soft and silky, a strange juxtaposition with the collection of sharp, curved battle axe blades fanned out above it. I didn't touch either, backing away and pivoting toward a seating area with high-backed, tufted, black chairs surrounding a waist-high, rectangular slab of obsidian.

I approached it, curious as to its purpose. It wasn't a table. There was a long ebony table on the far side of the room lined with straight, solemn chairs. Besides, it was too narrow, and it had a curious groove running the length of it.

I held my breath as I ran my fingers across the top of the smooth stone. Maybe it was a religious altar? I hadn't recalled much about Vandar beliefs, although I did remember something about their adherence to ancient mythology and old gods. Did they believe that warriors went to a special afterlife with their warlike gods? Maybe this was a monument to their gods?

As my fingers slid across the cold stone, I felt an indentation, which I instinctively pressed. Instantly, flames burst from the long groove at the top, and I jumped back.

"It's a fireplace." I shook my head, almost laughing at myself. At least, I hadn't uttered my theories about it being a religious altar to anyone.

The flames dancing above the black stone gave out a startling amount of heat, and I held my hands to them. I hadn't realized how cold I'd been until the fire began to warm me. It made sense that a vessel that was cavernous and forged from hard metal wouldn't be the warmest and coziest place, but how did all the Vandar run around in nothing but those strips of leather that made up their kilts? They didn't look cold, whereas I was still in the flight suit that covered me from head to toe, and I was shivering.

"It's the shock," I reminded myself. "You've been taken captive by some renegade aliens who think you know something that can help them in their revenge plot."

It was ridiculous that I would know anything that could help them find the other Vandar, even if I had any intention of betraying the Valox allies. I might feel a twinge of sympathy for these lost Vandar who'd grown up feeling rejected, but raging against your own kind and taking hostages wasn't exactly the way to be welcomed home with open arms.

I stood as close as I could to the fire without actually burning, and I rubbed my arms briskly. The heat helped my muscles uncoil and my pulse slow. "Think, Sloane. You're Valox. You got yourself into this mess. You can get yourself out."

My job within the resistance had consisted of flying and shooting. We'd done some rudimentary training on being captured when I'd first joined, but it had been pretty basic, and it had been based around the presumption that our captors would be Zagrath. I hadn't prepared for being taken by the Vandar, and more specifically a mutinous offshoot of the Vandar who held none of their people's alliances. How was I supposed to negotiate my way out, if I didn't even know if these Vandar could be trusted not to put me out an airlock?

I thought about Raas Ronnan and the way he'd looked at me. Okay, I was pretty sure his main interest in me wasn't in venting me into space, but he hadn't been serious about me joining him in bed, had he? That had to be a Vandar figure of speech, right?

I'd heard whispers of how Raas Kratos had come to take a human bride, but since they were happily mated I'd always thought those were just dramatic stories meant to make the Vandar seem even scarier. Even if she had been his war prize, she'd gone with him willingly, which was a far cry from what was going on here.

I gulped and tried not to remember how my heart had raced when Ronnan had touched me and how my mouth had gone dry when he'd been pressed up so close to me I could feel the heat of his body radiating into me. There was no way I should react to him like that, especially since he was an arrogant warlord with a serious vengeance problem who was holding me against my will.

"Come on, Sloane." I gave myself a hard shake to rid myself of the unwanted tingles the memory of the Raas provoked. "You need to be thinking of escape, not wondering what he's packing under that leather skirt."

My cheeks warmed, and I glanced around as if there was anyone around to hear me. If Cassie and Thea were here they'd be scolding me for getting distracted—again. The same skills that made me a great pilot who could react quickly also made my mind jump all over the place. It was why I listened to the vintage Earth rock they hated.

I grinned as the realization hit me. I didn't need the earbuds that had been taken from me outside the *oblek* to focus, and there was no one to complain about my horrible singing here.

"It's the eye of the tiger, it's the thrill of the fight," I sang to myself as I crossed to the far wall that was draped in a heavy, gray curtain. I fumbled with the fabric at one end until I found a panel on the wall, which I pressed. The curtains fell back to reveal floor-to-ceiling glass and a wide swath of black space.

I gazed out and took a deep breath. I was as determined to get back out there and return to my mission as these lost Vandar were to exact their revenge. "May the best woman win."

CHAPTER
SEVEN

"I'm telling you, she wouldn't miss a check-in like this, Thea." The woman with wavy, blue hair falling in her eyes jogged down the low-ceilinged corridor after her friend, ducking her head to avoid a loose pipe hissing steam. The scent of fuel and damp earth was pervasive in the underground complex, as was the cold, although both women wore jumpsuits that covered them from head to toe.

"It's Sloane." Thea shoved up her sleeves and flipped a glossy, jet-black braid off her shoulder. "She probably got distracted listening to Joan Jeff and lost track of the time."

"I think it's Joan *Jett*." Cassie shot the engineer a side-eye glance. "And you know she's never failed to check in when she was scheduled to, even when she was in full rock-out mode. She may have a weird thing for vintage Earth music, but she's great at her job."

"The job that she doesn't really have anymore?"

Cassie blew an errant wave of hair from her forehead. "She can still be a pilot. The resistance might not be needed to blow imperial fighters from the sky anymore, but there's still work to be done repairing the mess the Zagrath made. We've both been busy since the empire was defeated."

"Running supply missions to the planets no longer under imperial control." Thea dodged a pair of resistance fighters in dark flight suits who took up most of the narrow underground corridor. "Sloane isn't interested in doing that because she doesn't believe the war is over."

Cassie made a face and shushed her friend. "Don't say that so loud."

"It's no secret." Thea walked from the tunnel into a wide hangar bay filled with spaceships in various states of repair. "She's told anyone who will listen that she's convinced there are pockets of imperial soldiers hiding out and rebuilding their forces."

"That's not outside the realm of possibility. The Zagrath did collapse pretty quickly. Who's to say they didn't prepare for something like this, and had some sort of place to hide out and regroup?"

Thea shook her head as she strode toward a chunky, gunmetal-gray vessel, with an open panel on the side. "You really think the empire thought they'd ever be defeated? They controlled so much of the sector I don't think it even occurred to them that the Valox resistance and the Vandar would join forces with rebellions on some of the planets to overthrow them."

Cassie shrugged. "Maybe you're right, but you know Sloane can't let the war go so easily."

Thea stopped when she reached the ship. She released a breath. "I was as crushed as anyone when Leo was killed. I'd served as his engineer on a bunch of missions. He was a great pilot, and an even better person. But chasing the ghosts of the Zagrath isn't going to bring him back for her."

"Grief doesn't always make sense."

Thea nodded before turning her attention to the exposed wiring of the ship. "The Valox leaders won't approve many more of these pointless search missions of hers, so I hope she gets it out of her system soon."

Cassie muttered something about Thea and tough love before leaving the engineer and walking up the ship's open ramp. She needed to input new coordinates for an upcoming mission to deliver medical supplies and medicine to a colony that had been relocated to a deserted planet by the Zagrath. As a navigator, her job had become more straightforward now that the Valox resistance wasn't planning complicated sneak attacks and routes to avoid any imperial contact.

She loved her job, and her fellow rebels were like family, but she understood Sloane's reluctance to move forward with her life. They'd trained to fight in a rebellion. Now that the rebellion was over, what were they fighting for anymore? Some of the fighters had already returned to their homes, but like Sloane and Thea, Cassie didn't have family waiting for her.

The Valox resistance was her family, and it was slowly disbanding. The thought of one day leaving Sloane and Thea, her best friends since the moment they'd met at Valox training, made her stomach churn and tears sting the backs of her eyes. They were like sisters to her. She couldn't imagine life without them.

Cassie sank into the pilot's seat in the cockpit and glanced out the front of the ship to where pilots were crossing the oil-stained floor and deck crew were waving vessels toward open runways. She'd even miss the dingy, rebellion headquarters that was hidden on the surface of Galdon V, although she wouldn't object to a place with reliable hot water and better cooks. Maybe now that they didn't need to hide anymore, they could upgrade their facilities to a planet that wasn't so remote and lacking in luxuries.

She swallowed a lump in her throat. If they even bothered keeping a headquarters.

Shaking her head and focusing on the task at hand, Cassie swiped her fingers across the console to bring up the ship's navigational log. She'd already plotted out the fastest route, accounted for a stop on Hebron to pick up supplies, and calculated the amount of fuel needed. Now she just had to input the coordinates, wait for Thea to make the necessary repairs, and the pilot would be good to go.

When she heard footsteps behind her, she didn't bother glancing back at Thea. "I know. I know. You're already done with the repairs. Give me two seconds, and I'll have the navigational systems upgraded and ready to roll."

"Forget the supply mission."

Cassie spun around. Thea stood grim-faced next to one of the Valox commanders.

"What's wrong? Does the colony not need the supplies anymore?"

Thea pressed her lips into a hard line as she shook her head. "You were right. Sloane didn't get distracted."

Cassie's heart plummeted, as the Valox commander cleared his throat. "Sloane's ship was found abandoned."

"Abandoned?" Her voice cracked.

"It appears your friend was taken." He slid his gaze to Thea and then back to Cassie. "And since you two know her better than anyone, you're going to lead the team to find her."

CHAPTER
EIGHT

Ronnan

"She can't escape?" I asked Kaiven, when he joined me in my strategy room.

My battle chief inclined his head slightly, as if this was an unnecessary question. "Not unless she can fight off the two Vandar raiders guarding the door."

I stood on the other side of my desk, facing him with my arms braced wide on the polished stone that gleamed as dark as the rest of the ebony interior. My compact strategy room held little but my desk, a glittering star chart on the ceiling, and a narrow glass wall overlooking space. It was where I came to plot and plan. It was not designed for comfort or contemplation. I had my quarters for that. Until now.

I questioned my own impulsive decision to keep the female in my private quarters. It was true we had no brig—there was no point, since the Vandar did not take prisoners—but I could have left her in Kaiven's *oblek*. It was a space designed for interrogating enemies.

The thought of the small female being strung up with his chains or lashed to the walls with his straps made both anger and desire spike within me. If there was anyone who would punish the female for not being more forthcoming, it would be me. But I did not intend to use such blunt instruments as Kaiven's weapons.

"Are you sure it's a good idea to keep a captive, Raas?" Ayden stood at the glass wall, turning as he spoke and taking slow steps to face me.

"If she's truly an ally of the Vandar, then she's more than a captive. She's leverage."

Aydan grunted. He didn't agree with me. "Do we need leverage? We aren't coming to negotiate. We're coming to demand."

"Everything is a negotiation," I said, repeating the words I'd heard from my mother, who was shrewder than my father ever gave her credit for being. "Even a battle is a negotiation with blood."

Kaiven nodded vigorously. "And if the Vandar do not meet our demands, their blood will run like the silver rivers on Selk."

I thought of the wild rivers that cut through the land we'd left behind, water rushing over iridescent stone that made it appear as if it was carved from glittering silver. My heart squeezed at memories of the only home I'd ever known, and all we'd left behind to exact vengeance for our fathers.

"Did the female give you any information?" My *majak* asked, cutting through my memories and jerking back to the dark room that was quiet, but for the rumbling of the ship beneath our feet.

I would not admit that she'd given us almost nothing, or that I believed her knowledge of the Vandar to be limited. My reasons for keeping her were already tenuous. I did not need my *majak* to tell me what I already knew. Keeping the female was a risk we didn't need, but I could not force myself to release her. Not yet. "I will continue the questioning privately."

Kaiven's lips curled into a knowing grin, but Ayden frowned.

"You are claiming her as a spoil of war?" my *majak* asked. "Like Kratos with his human mate?"

I shook my head. I had not left home and traveled across the galaxy to take a human mate. If we were to redeem our bloodline, my raiders needed to take Vandar brides. That included me most of all. We did not have the luxury of the Raases who'd taken humans. They were full-blooded Vandar with a legitimate claim to their positions. I was already a mixed blood exile. I could not indulge in more diluting of my Vandar line. "You know my intentions when it comes to a mate."

"To claim a Vandar female," Aydan made a face. "If we can find them."

"We will find them," I said with more confidence than I felt. "The Vandar are no longer operating in secret."

"That doesn't mean they've revealed the location of their hidden colonies." My *majak* leveled a solemn gaze at me. "Even our fathers didn't know the coordinates of the hidden colonies where the females and families were kept safe."

"We might find the hordes," Kaiven added. "But Vandar warbirds do not carry females."

Ayden folded his arms over his chest, the strap holding his shoulder armor cutting into his pectoral muscle. "They will die before they reveal their secrets. Just as we would."

"That is where the female captive comes in," I told them both as I came from behind my desk. "They might be more willing to talk if a human female is in danger, especially one who fought with them against the empire."

Ayden didn't look convinced, but he rocked back on his heels. "We searched her ship. What she says appears to be true. The vessel has been in many battles and the battle logs record fights against the empire, although there are no identifiers to connect the ship to the Valox."

"If it is a resistance group, it makes sense that their ships wouldn't be easily identified." My battle chief gave an almost approving nod. "Is it customary for rebel groups to use such fragile females in battle?"

"She is a pilot," I said. "Not a warrior who engages in hand-to-hand combat."

My battle chief shrugged. "She would have shot down enemy ships."

I crossed my arms over my own chest. "The effort to take down the empire did not succeed until the Vandar joined it."

"Maybe because they used females to fight their battles," Kaiven suggested.

Ayden slid his gaze first to Kaiven, then to me. "I believe it is unwise to underestimate this female. Even if she is human, she is a trained pilot who fought against the empire."

I cocked my head at my *majak*, the corners of my mouth twitching. "Do you think I am in danger with her in my quarters?"

"Do I think the small creature will overpower you?" Ayden returned my wry smile. "Of course not, Ronnan. You are a Raas of the Vandar. The Kyrie Vandar."

Kaiven growled at this. Being the Lost Vandar made us even fiercer and more determined. We were warriors to be feared.

"That doesn't mean she isn't dangerous," Ayden said, giving me a pointed gaze. "She is a female who is not without her allure."

Had my *majak* noticed my reaction to her? He was my closest friend. If anyone knew me and what stirred my deepest desires, it was Ayden. Or was he merely giving the same counsel he would if our ship had taken any female onboard?

"I have not come all this way to be distracted by a female." I crossed to the glass and scoured the endless night of the sky. "Much less, a human." I clasped the hilt of my battle axe, letting my fingers caress the carved iron that was cool to the touch. My skin burned as I thought about the female in my quarters. I could not afford to lose my way when we'd come so far and were so close. As much as she might have awakened dormant desires in me, I couldn't allow my weakness to push me off course. Our mission was still revenge, and our target had not changed.

"What are your orders, Raas?" Kaiven asked. "Aside from the insignificant Valox ship, we have picked up no other vessels, and we have no leads on where the hordes might be hiding."

I flinched at his assessment of our progress since we'd entered Vandar territory, hating that he was right. We were no closer to challenging the Vandar than when we'd began our mission.

"I will find out more from the human." I spun around, the straps of my kilt slapping my thighs. "If she knows anything about the Vandar, I will discover it."

"You may use my *oblek*, Raas," my battle chief said, the thrill evident in his voice. "Or I can bring my devices to your quarters."

I shook my head, my heart already pounding at the thought of questioning the female. "I won't need them. I plan to charm the information from her."

Both warriors stared at me, their startled expressions stopping me as I strode toward the door.

"You don't believe I can charm a female?"

Kaiven shook his head before stopping himself and clearing his throat. "It isn't that you cannot, Raas, but your interactions with females have always been..."

I thought of the nights my horde had entertained themselves in the pleasures houses and how bored I'd been by the pretty alien females. Paying for pleasure provided no challenge, and I'd dispatched with my pleasurers with an efficiency that had drawn stifled laughs.

I slid my gaze to my *majak*. "You doubt my charm as well?"

He met my eyes. "Charm is not what made you Raas. It was your ferocity in battle and your ruthlessness in pursuit."

Ayden was right. I had not become a warlord of the Vandar because I was skilled at seduction. "Then I will not pretend to be what I am not." I stomped the rest of the way to the door and glanced back at them when it slid open. "And if she resists me, she will learn just how ruthless and ferocious a Raas of the Vandar can be."

CHAPTER
NINE

Sloane

I didn't hear the door slide open behind me, but the heavy boots thumping against the floor made me whirl around.

Raas Ronnan strode toward me, his eyes blazing and the strips of leather that made up his kilt flapping. As intense as his gaze was, it was impossible not to notice his powerful and muscular thighs and the beads of sweat glistening off his broad chest and ridged stomach. He heaved in breaths, and I wondered if he'd run through the ship to reach his quarters —or me.

The Vandar warlord stopped in front of me, but so close that his heat pulsed into me, and I had to tilt my head to meet his eyes.

"How do you find the living quarters of a Vandar Raas?"

I fought the urge to back away, although I would have only bumped into the glass wall. How was I supposed to answer that? It wasn't like I'd seen other Vandar sleeping quarters. "Nice?"

He grunted, his gaze never leaving mine as his pupils widened so that his eyes were like fathomless pools of black. "Have you reconsidered?"

My mouth was so dry I could barely scratch out a response. "Reconsider what?"

"Being more forthcoming about how much you know about the Vandar."

My heart stuttered and my mouth dropped open. "I told you what I know, which isn't much."

The Vandar with alabaster hair and brown scruff dusting his cheeks made disapproving noises in the back of his throat. "You can't expect me to believe that the Vandar would be your ally, but you would know nothing about them." He reached up and brushed an errant strand of hair from my forehead. "A top pilot like you must be privy to intelligence about your partners in battle."

Shitty shitty shit shit. My own words were coming back to bite me in the butt. Why had I felt the need to brag about my battle record? It had been true—I did have the most kills of almost any pilot in the resistance—but now I'd made myself sound like someone who called the shots, which was definitely not true.

"That's not the way the Valox resistance works. Pilots aren't in the inner circle when it comes to strategy or battle plans, and if anyone knows the scoop on the Vandar, it isn't me."

He tilted his head slowly as if studying my face for tells. Well, he could study all he wanted. I wasn't lying. I flew when and where I was told. The only way a rebel force maintained its secrecy was by sharing information on a "no one needs to know" basis.

"I promise you I'm telling the truth." My voice trembled as I spoke, but I forced myself to hold his gaze.

"That is exactly what a warrior trained in resistance and subterfuge would say." He traced one finger down the side of my face. "How can I be sure you aren't lying to me to keep the Vandar safe?"

"Why would I do that? The Vandar don't need protection from me. They're the biggest badasses in the galaxy."

This got a reaction from him. A muscle ticked in his jaw and his eyes narrowed ever so slightly. "You do not think they need protection from me and my horde?"

Fuck me. I walked into that one. I took a breath to steady myself. "I didn't mean you."

He reached behind me and pulled my hair from its ponytail before tangling one hand in it and cupping the back of my head in his palm. "You didn't answer my question, female. Do you think I'm dangerous?"

His tail wound around my calves as he closed the distance between us. It wasn't hard to believe he'd descended from wild predators who'd once stalked creatures on the open plains as he lowered his head and tipped my head back so he could inhale the skin of my exposed throat. He was so much bigger and stronger than me that any thoughts of running or fighting him off were instantly dispelled. He could kill me with the snap of my neck and catch me without breaking a sweat. If I was under any illusion that these Vandar weren't deadly—maybe more deadly than the ones who had been feared throughout the galaxy—that was shattered as the warlord held me with one hand as if I was a ragdoll.

"Yes," I choked out the word as he grasped me and breathed in my scent like he was going to be hunting me.

He leaned back so he could eye me hungrily. "Then why do you continue to resist my questioning."

"I'm not." My chest heaved and my voice was high and breathy, which sounded foreign to my ears. "I've told you everything I know."

"Mmmm." He used his free hand to drag one finger down the length of my throat and tease the neckline of my flight suit so that the zipper slid down further. "Maybe you have, maybe you haven't. There are ways to know which it is."

Fear danced along my spine. "I'll take a lie detector test or drink a serum if you have it."

My plea sounded desperate, and I wasn't surprised when a cool smile crossed his face.

"A serum?" He actually laughed, the low sound rumbling into me. "The Vandar do not use such things to evoke the truth. We prefer more ancient methods."

My mind went to the brutal weapons that had hung on the walls of the dark room I'd first entered, their edges sharp and their spikes piercing. "It won't help your cause if you torture one of the Vandar's allies."

He licked his bottom lip and shook his head, sliding one hand down to the small of my back and pressing me to him. "What gave you the idea I would torture you?"

Confusion swirled in my brain and made me so lightheaded I was barely aware that my feet were lifting from the floor and skimming the shiny surface as he propelled me backward. "You said ancient methods. That usually means torture."

"Then you don't know the Vandar well." He arched a brow. "Maybe I should believe you, after all, female, although that wouldn't be as much fun."

"You should believe me." My heart hammered in my chest as I was walked up a step and the backs of my legs bumped something soft. I now understood that the ancient methods of extracting information had nothing to do with axes or blades, but a part of me wished I was back in that darkened torture chamber instead of being dragged to the alien warlord's bed.

It was true that Raas Kratos had taken his human mate in exchange for sparing her sister's imperial transport ship, but I didn't remember the Vandar being known for taking females against their will. Sure, they were brutal warriors who pillaged and raided, but Raas Ronnan wasn't serious, was he?

Then I swallowed hard as I remembered that he wasn't like the Vandar of this sector. I couldn't assume he would act the same way they had. The only thing I knew for sure was that he wanted to find them as part of a generational act of vengeance, and I was the only clue he had to finding them.

His hand slid to my hip, gripping it and rooting me in place as he relaxed his grip on my head, moving his fingers through my hair again so slowly it was almost mesmerizing. "You're sure you don't want to tell me what I want to know?"

I considered making up something—anything—to appease him, but when the information didn't pan out as true, I feared it would be even worse for me. "I can't tell you something I don't know."

His gaze swept across my face before he pressed his lips together and nodded. "I admire your courage, female. It is foolish and pointless, but I admire it."

Then he released his grip on my hip and pushed me back. I hit the bed and bounced as he remained at the foot of it. His gaze was pure heat as he unhooked the metal studded belt that ringed his waist and it hit the floor with a thud. I scuttled away from him as he removed a leather strap that crossed his chest, lowering it and the battle axe attached to it to the floor and kicking them to the center of the room.

Seeing the axe slide across the floor made me glance up at the looming headboard of axes. I returned my gaze to him, panic surging through me as he started to loosen his kilt. I leapt up and lunged for the headboard, praying that I could loosen one.

My hands clamped around a handle, and I pulled as hard as I could. It wouldn't budge. From close up, I could see that they were welded together. My shoulders sagged as I turned back around, but I clenched my fists and readied myself for a fight.

The warlord looked even more striking and terrifying as he eyed me with raw hunger, and his fingers and the tip of his tail twitched as if he was about to pounce. "There is nothing that brings a Vandar more pleasure than a good fight."

I'd accidentally dabbled in Vandar foreplay? Just fucking great, Sloane.

CHAPTER
TEN

Ronnan

Before I could see how far the female would go in her attempt to fight me, the door opened, and Ayden entered, along with several other Vandar carrying trays.

"I thought our guest might need some nourishment." His eyebrows lifting at the sight of the female standing on the bed and yanking at the headboard was the only indication he was startled.

I turned and walked to him, leaving my discarded armor on the floor, but snatching up my battle axe. I had no intention of mauling the female, but she didn't know that, and I preferred not to fight her off while she wielded my weapon.

"I see your charm is working as expected," my *majak* muttered as I passed him.

I spun the wooden handle of my axe, following the savory scents of food to the table. "I decided to leave charm as a last resort."

Ayden choked back a laugh as he cut his gaze to the female standing on my bed. "Apparently."

I plucked a warm roll from a metal bowl and took a bite, the yeasty dough pillowy and soft in my mouth. I dropped my voice so only Ayden could hear me. "I was not going to claim the female, *majak*." I snuck a glance at the human as she eyed us from her position on the bed. Her hair was wild, and her chest rose and fell as she glared at me. It was hard to stifle my carnal urges when she looked like she wished to engage in battle right there on my bed. "You know I have never taken a female against her will."

"Yes, but we've never taken a female on board our warbird, either."

I twitched one shoulder in acknowledgment of this fact as I discarded it. "It matters not. I am a Raas of the Vandar. I do not need to force a female."

Now Ayden shrugged. It was no secret we paid for pleasurers, but that was different. As raiders, we had little time to woo females as we traveled, therefore we were frequent patrons of the skilled females who plied their craft of seduction. Still, it was their choice and they set their own boundaries, which their madams ensured we did not cross. I also enforced this respect among my horde. None of my warriors would take what was not given freely by a female or they would suffer severe consequences. The Vandar only raided for ships and cargo—and now revenge—not for females, despite the tales that had been spread by the empire.

"Have your less-than-charming interrogation techniques gleaned any new information?"

I frowned, giving my head a curt shake. "Not yet. She is fiercer than she looks."

The edges of my *majak's* mouth trembled. "I can see that." He slid his gaze to the battle axe I held in one hand. "Should I remove your weapon before she slits your throat while you sleep?"

I stopped chewing for a moment as a forbidden thrill went through me at the thought of sleeping in the same bed as the female, then I considered my most trusted advisor's warning and handed him my axe. "This is why you are my *majak*."

"Your battle chief would prefer she be safely tied up in his *oblek*," Ayden reminded me.

I stole another glance at the female, who'd stopped her futile attempts to free a weapon from the ones soldered together above my bed. "For now, we will try my way."

My *majak* stifled another chuckle, coughing to mask it. He waved for the other Vandar, who'd delivered the food and arranged it down the length of the table, to follow him as he backed toward the door. "Then we will leave you to your strategy."

I ignored the doubt in his tone as he led the others from my quarters and the door slid shut behind them. I'd been sure that the female would have talked when she believed her virtue was at risk, but she'd chosen instead to attempt to fight me. It had been absurd—even if she'd been successful in loosening an axe she would have been no match for me—but it had been brave. It made me wonder if she was telling the truth and she knew nothing more than she'd already told me about the Vandar in this sector or if she was a more devoted rebel than I'd anticipated.

"Vaes," I called to her, as I took a seat at the end of the table. "You should eat while the food is hot."

She hesitated, narrowing her eyes at me but not descending from my bed.

I held my arms wide. "I have no weapon. You are safe."

She snorted out a laugh as she mumbled something about me not needing an axe. She was right, of course. I was deadly without any weapon, but I also had no intention of laying a hand on her. Not without her wishing it. But that wasn't something I wanted her to know. Not yet.

I held her gaze across the room. "I give you my word as a Kyrie Vandar upon the memory of the old gods and the name of Lokken, that you will be safe with me while we eat."

She considered this, nibbling the edge of her lip before she huffed out a breath and tramped across the bed. "Fine, but only because I know how serious you Vandar take your ancient gods." She stepped down from the bed and then paused. "Unless that's something you abandoned when you were exiled."

Irritation flared within me at the thought that we would abandon the gods. It had not been the Kyrie Vandar who had done the forsaking. We had been the ones cast out.

I suppressed a rumble in my throat. "We did not abandon the gods. I swear on the soul of my beloved mother, you will not be harmed."

She appraised me and then nodded, continuing her walk across the room and taking a seat in the middle of one of the long sides.

I was amused she didn't take the seat of honor at the far end. I inclined my head toward it. "You do not wish to sit across from me?"

She took a roll and bit into it, her eyes closing in obvious pleasure as she chewed. When she swallowed, she opened her eyes. "That seems like a seat that should be saved for someone else."

There was no one else in the room and no one would be joining us, but she was right that that would have been the seat for a Raisa, the mate of the Raas. Had she sensed this and avoided it because she knew as well as I did that she was merely a prisoner of war, and this game between us would lead to nothing?

"That is where my Raisa will sit," I told her, curious as to her reaction.

"Do you have a Raisa?" She froze in the middle of scooping a ruddy-hued stew onto her plate, her nose wrinkling as if she'd smelled something foul.

I shook my head quickly, eager to dispel the look of disgust on her face. Why did I care so much what this human female thought? Didn't I want her to believe me ruthless and without scruples? Shouldn't I wish to perpetuate the reputation of the Vandar as merciless and hard-hearted? Not if it meant she looked at me like that, I didn't.

"I have no Raisa." I reached for a jug of wine and poured some into my goblet, then I motioned for her to hand me her empty one. "I am unmated." I slid my eyes to the chair at the end. "So, you may sit there, if you wish."

She handed me her chunky, metal goblet, her gaze not meeting mine. "I'm good right here."

I poured the crimson wine and passed her glass back to her, her small fingers brushing mine when she took it. Heat sizzled up my arm, but I ignored it as we ate in silence. As she ate with impressive speed, I wondered how long it had been since her last meal.

"Do the Valox not feed you well?" I asked as I watched her drain her goblet.

She looked up at me with wide eyes, as if she'd been caught doing something naughty. "Sorry. I guess I'm used to eating fast. When you work in the resistance, you eat a lot of ration packs, and when there's actually hot food, it goes quickly. Sometimes, you eat fast, or not at all."

"I do not mind." I refilled her goblet, knowing that humans would not be accustomed to the strength of Vandar wine and hoping that her thirst loosened her tongue. "The Vandar appreciate voracious appetites."

I noticed the swell of her cleavage that I'd exposed when I'd unzipped the neckline of her flight suit. My cock thickened as I envisioned what else the zipper might reveal if it could be coaxed lower. I could not take her for a Raisa, but that didn't mean I could not enjoy a taste of the female while she was in my possession.

I took a sip of my own wine as I watched her drink as if she'd been trudging across a desert for days. Maybe her tongue would not be all that would be loosened.

CHAPTER
ELEVEN

Sloane

I took another gulp of wine, humming Joan Jett's "Crimson and Clover" to myself. Sure, I was thirsty, but I also needed to douse some of the spice from the Vandar food. I wasn't surprised that the brutal aliens liked their food strong, but after living off bland ration packs and watery soups dished out en masse to the resistance fighters, the aggressive spices made my eyes water.

Despite the spice, the alien food was good. Not exactly gourmet, but the hearty stew was filled with chunks of meat that melted in my mouth, and the bread... I paused my humming to moan as I bit into another soft roll then glanced furtively at Ronnan. The last thing I wanted was for him to hear my sounds of pleasure and get the wrong idea.

Even though he looked at me over the top of his goblet, my sounds hadn't merited a response, so I returned my attention to my plate, which I'd almost cleaned. I tried to ignore the feel of his gaze on me or the heat stirring in my core knowing that he was watching me.

Why did the Vandar provoke such a mess of emotions in me? He was my captor. I should despise him. I should *not* have traitorous feelings about the gorgeous alien or wonder what it would be like to tumble around in bed with someone with such a fiery temper.

Leo had been so even-keeled and patient—the polar opposite of this impatient and threatening Vandar—and our intimate time together had been wonderful, but not combustible. There had never been the fear of losing control or losing myself. With Ronnan, I had the feeling I would lose everything.

I took another swig of wine to wash down the yeasty roll and sat back in my chair. I'd eaten so quickly, I'd barely noticed the warm tingles radiating up my hands and feet—or the fact that my lips had gone numb. I touched my fingers to my mouth, my movements sluggish.

I lifted my gaze to the Raas, who was still observing me. "Did you drug the food?"

He blinked a few times in rapid succession. "No. I ate the same food as you and drank the same wine."

Right. I dropped my gaze to his plate, which was also nearly cleaned. We'd eaten from the same bowls and drunk wine from the same carafe. Then why did I feel so lightheaded, and why did he look completely sober?

"You drank as if you were dying of thirst," he said as if he knew the questions that swirled through my mind. "Vandar wine is potent, and you are much smaller than any Vandar."

I opened my mouth to argue that I could hold my liquor just fine, but my head was swimming. Instead, I blurted out, "You think just because you're bigger than me you're in charge?"

He angled his head. "I believe I am in charge because I am Raas, and you are my captive." He smiled at me. "I just happen to be larger than you."

"Yeah, well, you're larger than everyone," I muttered, flapping a hand at him. "And don't think I'm not well aware that you're large everywhere."

The moment the words left my mouth I wished I could take them back. I closed my eyes and winced. Why had I said that out loud? "Fuck, Sloane. Why can't you shut up?"

"Don't shut up on my account."

My eyes flew open. Wait, had I told myself to shut up out loud? From the grin on the Vandar warlord's face, it was clear I had. Fuck, fuck, fuck. "Ignore me. Please. I'm rambling."

"I enjoy hearing what's going through your mind. I've encountered few human females before and none who were warriors. You're more intriguing and entertaining than I expected."

I glared at him. "I'm not here for your entertainment."

"Since you're my prisoner, I don't think you get a say in deciding your purpose." His smile slipped. "As you have pointed out, I am considerably larger than you." His gaze darted to his bed. "And you've learned that there are no weapons you can use to fight me."

A chill passed through me followed by a shiver of unwanted pleasure. "That doesn't mean I won't try."

He leaned forward and his straight platinum hair fell forward to shadow his face. "I'm counting on it, female."

Even though my heart pounded, I couldn't help snapping back. "My name is Sloane, not female."

He gave a lazy shrug. "Sloane, then. I would expect nothing less than a fight from a member of the rebellion."

I braced myself. He'd kept his word and allowed me to eat without touching me, but our meal was finished. Should I run? I scanned the space, but as I'd discovered before, there was nowhere to run and no way for me to open the doors. Even if I could, I'd seen the guards posted outside when the Vandar had left after delivering the food.

Instead of pouncing on me or even standing from the table, Ronnan fell back in his chair. "How old were you when you decided to join the rebellion? Is it common for human females in this sector to become fighters?"

I was taken aback by his sudden shift in tone and subject, but I was also grateful he wasn't eyeing me like I was one of the dishes on the table. My brain still felt fuzzy, but I was shrewd enough to know that if the Vandar was talking he couldn't be doing other things like chasing me or pinning me down in bed.

"I always wanted to be a pilot, but I was born on one of the planets the empire had taken over and ground down so that no one could do anything but eke out enough to survive. My parents worked themselves to the bone, but barely kept us all fed. I guess I didn't have much reason to stay, when I met a resistance pilot, and he told me I could be trained to fly and fight the empire."

"You left your home to fight?" He gave me an appreciative nod. "You are not so different from the Vandar, then."

"I had no reason to stay. My parents had died from illness. I had no other family, and I hated the empire for how they'd ruined the lives of everyone on my planet." A surge of rage overpowered my muddled brain. "Joining the Valox wasn't a sacrifice. It was a privilege."

The warlord growled his approval. "You claimed you have the most kills of any rebel fighter. They taught you to fly so well?"

"The resistance might be underground, but they managed to train up a sizable force just by recruiting people from planets the empire had ruined." Pride made my chest swell. "We have some of the best fighters in the galaxy. Better than any imperial hack."

"Purpose gave you power." Ronnan's voice was a velvet purr as he eyed me without moving from his reclined position in his chair. "Now that the empire has been defeated, what will become of your resistance?"

"I don't think they're gone," I said, before I could stop myself. "Something as powerful and huge as the empire wouldn't be destroyed so easily. I think there are imperial forces in hiding just waiting for us to disband and become complacent. I can feel it."

His relaxed posture stiffened. "The resistance doesn't think the empire has been destroyed?"

"Oh, they do. It's just me who doesn't. Not even my best friends in the resistance, Cassie and Thea, believe me and they're as loyal as they come." I cursed under my breath. "I shouldn't have said any of that. Forget you heard anything."

"About your best friends being named Cassie and Thea or about your theory that no one believes?"

I frowned, suspecting he was mocking me.

"You do not need to worry about me revealing your secrets." He spread his arms wide. "Who would I tell?"

I blew out a breath. "You don't need to worry about me telling yours, either."

"I am not." He pushed back his chair and the legs scraped across the floor. "You would have to leave my ship to reveal my secrets."

My mouth fell open as he strode away from me, dropping his kilt as he walked and continuing naked into the attached bathroom, his tail swishing above his perfect, round ass cheeks. "And I have no intention of letting you go."

CHAPTER
TWELVE

Ronnan

I didn't look back as I unhooked my battle kilt from my waist and let it fall to the floor with a smack. I didn't need to. I could sense her gaze on me as I strode from the room, through the arched doorway, and into the bathing chamber. My tail swished behind me as my heart tripped and my fingers buzzed with the awareness that the female was watching.

A rumble built in my throat, and it became a growl of derision as I entered the dark room forged entirely from obsidian stone, that shone like the vast blackness of space. I breathed in the warm, spicy air that was thick with moisture, and tried to force thoughts of the female from my mind.

I should not care whether or not her gaze followed me or if she liked what she saw. I was a Raas of the Vandar, a warlord of the most fearsome warriors in the galaxy. I struck terror in the hearts of fighters. I should not be concerned by the thoughts of one insignificant, human female.

She is my captive anyway, I reminded myself. It does not matter what she likes or what she wishes. She is under my control.

I grunted at this thought, my cock swelling at the idea of controlling the small creature with the plump lips and wild hair. Then I remembered her lunging for the axes welded to my headboard, and a reluctant grin teased my lips. Controlling her might not be so easy.

"*That* is half the fun," I said to myself, as I kicked off my heavy boots and padded across the cold, ebony floor.

Steam billowed from the sunken pool in the center of the room, the perfume in the water making my nose twitch. The vents below the surface kept certain parts of the pool heated at all times, but I hadn't submerged myself in the healing waters since we'd closed in on Vandar space. I scanned the segmented pool, each of the four quadrants of the pool a distinct color and temperature meant to attend to various needs. Green algae from Candar Prime to heal wounds, blue ice crystals from Parisi to reduce swelling from bruises, crushed amber from Brikin IV to release memories, and crimson fire water from the depths of the Vralax caldera to elicit arousal and release inhibitions.

My bathing chamber had been modeled after the original Vandar design but modified with elements from our galaxy. Not even the Vandar of this sector possessed the powerful oils and minerals that made my bathing pool so magical.

After a brief hesitation, I chose the fiery red water and lowered myself quickly. I hissed in a breath as the bubbling water enveloped me with its heat, clenching my teeth until the burning sensation passed and my muscles began to unwind. I'd chosen the hottest water to release the tension that had bunched my shoulder muscles, but I was not ignorant of everything else that would be loosened once the fire water seeped into my skin.

The scent was strong and spicy, but not unpleasant, and I closed my eyes as I sank down and let the warmth cover me to my chin. The bubbles burst under my nose and tickled my scruffy cheeks. Beads of moisture trickled down my face and into my mouth, the taste sweeter than the smell.

When I opened my eyes, I tipped my head back to peer at the black ceiling with the pinpricks of blue light embedded in the shiny stone to mimic the stars from our home sky. This was not the night sky from the Vandar home world. It was the sky I'd grown up with far from Vandar space.

My gut tightened as I thought of how far I was from everything I knew. As much as I believed in our mission and burned with the vindication of our claim, a part of me felt like I was leading my horde into a battle that wasn't ours, against Vandar who had done nothing to wrong us.

I shook off these traitorous thoughts and straightened. The water sluiced from by body, red rivulets coursing down the curved muscles of my chest and across the dark, curling marks that would one day be completed when I found my true mate.

"A Vandar mate," I rasped, repeating the command my father had drilled into me, although the words sounded hollow as they echoed back to me in the dim chamber.

There were no other sounds but the water sloshing against the sides of the pool and my heavy breathing. My mind wandered to the female outside the room, and I cursed the flutter in my pulse. *Tvek.* Why did I find her so captivating? She was a small human who had no tail. Our Vandar fathers had not taken mates of their own species, but at least the Selkee females had been statuesque creatures, with silver hair that was luminescent in the moonlight. The human I'd captured was nothing like the imposing females of my mother's planet.

"She is brave," I conceded.

As spectacular as the Selkee females were, none of them would have considered taking up arms and fighting alongside males like Sloane had done. My heart thundered in my chest, no doubt aided by the heat of the water, as I imagined the human blasting imperial ships from the sky, her eyes flashing with some of the fury I'd seen when she'd challenged me.

Was it the challenge that drew me to her? Had I been searching for a fight for so long that I would even welcome one from a female I had no business engaging with? Or had it been too long since I'd buried my cock in a female who was not paid for her performance?

One thought drifted up in my mind as the water released my barriers like it was casting aside a thick blanket. I felt a kinship to Sloane. Even though she was human, and I was a Kyrie Vandar, I understood her need for vengeance, and I believed she understood mine.

But she is human, a voice in the back of my brain that sounded frighteningly like my father reminded me. *She can never be anything to you. Not a Raisa. Not a mate. Nothing.*

I growled as I plunged myself back under the scalding water. There were other things she could be to me aside from a mate or a Raisa or a captive.

"*Vaes!*" I bellowed, the sound of my booming voice reverberating off the stones.

There was no response, and the female didn't appear in the doorway as I'd expected. Stubborn creature.

"You can come of your own free will, or I can come drag you in here," I said, although I did not raise my voice this time. She would hear me.

When there was no sound in response, I scowled and prepared to leap from the water and fetch her. As I placed my hands on the edge of the pool, she materialized in the doorway. The scowl on her face matched mine, and her arms were crossed tight across her chest.

I fought the urge to laugh at her pointless show of defiance. "Choose a color."

CHAPTER
THIRTEEN

Sloane

I squinted at him, taking in the eerie bathroom that was only lit by dots of blue light twinkling in the ceiling. The Vandar wine hadn't worn off yet, so I didn't trust my fuzzy vision. Was he sitting in some type of thermal pool? From the steam rising from the surface and the aroma in the air, it sure looked like he was taking a bath and using scented oils. I hadn't known why he'd called me, but I hadn't expected this.

I wasn't used to seeing big, burly warriors lounging in steam baths. Then again, I wasn't used to fighters that bathed much at all. The barracks for the resistance had bathrooms that were utilitarian at best, with hot water that only occasionally worked. I'd gotten accustomed to taking lightning-quick showers, and plenty of the fighters skipped being doused in frigid water altogether. So, I guessed the spicy perfume I was inhaling was better than the stench of unwashed bodies.

"Choose a color," the Raas repeated, as I stood gaping at him.

I narrowed my eyes and glanced around the room in an attempt to figure out what he meant. What colors? I only saw black—black floor, black walls, a long, black counter with an equally long mirror above it. The wine had definitely muddled my mind because the Vandar wasn't making sense. "I don't understand."

He splashed one hand across the surface of the water. "The pools."

I'd been purposely avoiding looking anywhere south of his face, which meant I hadn't noticed that the water he was in was tinted. Then I saw that the pool wasn't one single, large pool, but four wedges of a circle. It wasn't easy to make out colors since it was so dimly lit and the lights illuminating the room were blue, but that didn't matter.

"You want me to get in there?" I shook my head and made no move toward him. "No, thanks."

Part of me would have loved to have luxuriated in a hot bath, but that would mean stripping down in front of the Raas, and I had no intention of doing that.

"You should bathe," he said, with no hint of impatience in his voice.

I blinked a few times. Did I smell? I suppressed the urge to raise my arm and sniff my armpit. I had been cooped up in a cramped cockpit for hours before they found me, and it might have been a day or two since I'd taken one of my speed showers. Had there been soap in the shower when I'd braved the ice water? I reminded myself that it didn't matter. "I'm good."

He tilted his head. "Is that your human way of saying you're disobeying my order?"

My heart stuttered in my chest. "You're ordering me to take a bath?"

"If that's what it takes." He shrugged as if it didn't really matter to him. "You may choose your water and get in on your own accord, or I will drag you in here with me." His gaze flicked up and down my body. "In your clothes."

I huffed out a breath and shot him a murderous look, but the potent wine had made me care less than I normally would. It wasn't like a Vandar warlord like Ronnan hadn't seen hundreds of naked females. One thing I remembered from the furtive stories about them before they'd become allies with the Valox was that the Vandar kept some of the pleasure planets in business.

Besides, I wasn't some giggling virgin. It wasn't uncommon to walk around the resistance barracks in underwear, even around the males. "I'm a Valox pilot who looks damn good naked."

Shit. Had I said that last part out loud? I didn't dare make eye contact with Ronnan to see if I had. Instead, I focused on stripping off my flight suit as quickly as possible. When I was only in my bra and panties, I hesitated. If I jumped in wearing them, I would have no dry underwear when I emerged. I cut my gaze to the flight suit in a heap on the floor. It was rough, scratchy fabric, and I did *not* relish the idea of going commando in it. The chafing would be real.

With a resigned sigh, I took off my bra and slid my panties down my legs, kicking them both to the side. I didn't look at the Vandar, as I made my way as quickly as I could to the wedge of the pool that was as far away from him as possible. I didn't hesitate in dropping down into the water so I could submerge my naked body as soon as I could.

"Fuck me!" I shrieked, as I hit the freezing water. I crossed my arms over my breasts as the skin pebbled painfully and my nipples puckered into fierce points.

"I am happy to oblige, but I am assuming this is another one of your human expressions."

I looked at Ronnan, who seemed to be stifling the urge to laugh. "You didn't tell me the water was ice."

"Not all of it is. You chose the blue pool, which is infused with blue ice crystals from Parisi. It is excellent for reducing swelling after a battle."

"Or making human popsicles." I shivered violently as I rubbed my arms.

"You could join me in here. The water in the red pool is hot."

I gave him a side eye glance. "I'm sure you'd love that, wouldn't you?"

"I would enjoy it more than watching you shiver. The Vandar do not get cold very easily, so that pool will feel even colder to you."

I cursed under my breath and tried to distract myself by singing Def Leppard, but my body was trembling so hard that I could barely get the word "sugar" out without stuttering.

"What are you doing?" Ronnan asked, wading through his pool until he was closer to me. "Aside from being unreasonably stubborn."

"I'm the right amount of stubborn for a prisoner of war," I managed to say. "I'm not supposed to do more than give you my name and rank. And the singing is helping distract me from the cold."

"Is it working?"

My teeth chattered, and my legs had gone numb.

He didn't wait for an answer. "I did not touch you while we ate. I will not touch you now while you bathe. I give you my word as a Raas of the Vandar."

I bobbed my head once, but my lips were too sluggish to move. The last thing I saw before my eyes rolled back in my head was Ronnan leaping naked from the water with everything on impressive display.

CHAPTER
FOURTEEN

Ronnan

S loane's eyelids fluttered and the arms wrapped around her chest went slack. She was passing out from the cold.

"*Tvek!*" I hoisted myself from the water as her eyes rolled up and she slid under the surface. I jumped into the pool, ignoring the bracing cold of the water, and scooped her into my arms. I ran up the pool's interior ramp and hurried to the orange-hued water. Dousing her in the blazing hot water right away would be too much of a shock to her system, but the gentle warmth of the amber infused water would raise her body temperature safely.

At least, I hoped it would. I knew nothing about human anatomy, except that I now knew they did not do well in freezing water.

I walked both of us into the orange water, my own limbs tingling from the shock of going from hot to frigid and now to warm. Sloane was still limp in my arms, so I bent my knees until she was submerged to her chin. Her hair floated behind her head, the brown frizz becoming long, straight, and silky when it was wet.

I should not look upon her naked body when she was unconscious, but it was impossible to avert my gaze when she was cradled in my arms. I'd glimpsed her when she'd disrobed, but she'd moved quickly. Now I could drink in the sight of her round breasts tipped with brown and the curious strip of neatly cropped hair between her legs.

I'd seen many alien females, but none so soft and unadorned. The females on Haralli had blue skin and wings that sprouted from their backs. The Grexians boasted double-jointed pelvises, and were entirely hairless, but covered in colorful tattoos. The Laxons has suckers for mouths and were dusted in a fine coat of translucent down. Although I'd encountered humans, their home world was nowhere near where the Kyrie Vandar had been raised, so they were as novel to me as an undiscovered species.

Her body might be curious to me, but I could not fight off the sense of connection to her that I'd felt earlier. Now that I gazed on her bare skin, I was overwhelmed with the sense that she was mine. Not only did I understand her warrior's heart, but I was also struck by an inexplicable sense of familiarity. I might not know humans, but I knew her.

A rough growl escaped from me as I watched the transparent orange water slide over her flesh, the blue tinge fading and her previous tan hue returning. I'd never wanted to possess anything more in my life, and my cock hardened as she stirred in my arms.

Now that she was warmed, I strode from the orange water and into the red. When I submerged her, she released a satisfied sigh that did nothing to help my aching cock.

She drowsily opened her eyes, her brow wrinkling as she peered at me. "What? Where?"

I slowly lowered her feet so that she was vertical, although I held the sides of her arms to keep her steady. "You insisted on freezing yourself, and you fainted."

Her eyes widened, she looked down at her naked body, then she ducked into the water until it reached her chin. "You brought me in here?"

"It was that, or watch you drown."

"Oh." Her gaze darted nervously. "Then thank you."

I grunted, releasing her arms and lowering myself fully, then backing away until I could hook my arms over the pool's ledge.

Sloane rubbed the side of her head. "It was so strange. When I was unconscious, I was dreaming, but the dream was a memory."

I didn't respond, deciding not to tell her that the amber water's power was that it released memories. If I revealed that, I might have to tell her that the fiery red water she was submerged in increased desire and lowered inhibitions. That was information I preferred to keep to myself in case I needed it later.

"I could have sworn I was back in the mud baths of Terrixia." She shook her head as she smiled. "I went there once when I had a few days of leave—with Leo."

"Leo?" An unfamiliar emotion prickled across my flesh.

She didn't meet my gaze. "My boyfriend. He was also a Valox pilot."

The thought of her with another male sent waves of fury pulsing through me. Was I jealous? She was my prisoner, I reminded myself. I had no claim on her, no matter what my body believed. Then my mind snagged on a word. "Was?"

Her faint smile vanished. "He died in battle."

I felt a shameful but brief rush of satisfaction at this. "At least he died a warrior's death."

Sloane pressed her lips together, finally meeting my gaze. "You're the first guy I've been attracted to since him." Then she gasped and slapped a hand over her mouth. "I can't believe I said that. Forget I said that."

I could not have forgotten she'd said that if I'd had my brain removed. "You are the first female I have been with since we left on our mission who has not been paid for. And the first human."

"Technically, you haven't *been* with me."

I lifted an eyebrow. "We are naked together."

She opened and closed her mouth before shaking her head firmly. "If you want to survive your mission, you can't be with me."

I eyed her, curious that the waters were loosening her tongue, and this is what she would confess. "Do you carry a disease?"

She stifled a laugh. "No, but that's a good idea. The next time I'm taken captive by a brutal warlord, I'll convince him I'm diseased."

I allowed my gaze to slip beneath the water to her naked body. "I doubt he would believe you."

"I may not be diseased, but I'm cursed. Everyone I care about dies. My parents died. My best friend on my home planet got sick and died. Leo died. Half of my squadron died during the final Zagrath battle." She looked away from me. "So, whatever happens, I can't fall for you. Unless you have a death wish."

"I do not have a death wish, although I do not fear death in battle." I stood and the water streamed from my chest "I cannot take a mate who is not Vandar, so we are both safe."

Her gaze faltered on the dark marks curling across my chest and over my shoulders. "Then we have a deal."

I heaved myself from the water in a single motion then dragged both hands over my face and down my hair so that droplets hit the floor behind me. I stood naked on the side of the pool, my eyes locked on hers as she openly stared at me. "We have a deal."

Then I turned and snatched a length of gray cloth from a rack, wrapping it around my waist as I scooped up my boots and stalked away from her, thinking that I'd just made the worst deal of my life.

CHAPTER
FIFTEEN

Sloane

I remained in the steaming water as the Raas left the bathroom. I couldn't see what he was doing, but it sounded like he was dressing in a hurry. The soft swish of the door and the ensuing quiet told me he'd left his quarters entirely.

"What the hell was that?" I muttered, sinking deeper beneath the water. I wasn't sure if I was more shocked by the fact that the Vandar had made a deal with me, or by the sight of the alien naked.

My cheeks were already warm from the water, but they flamed hotter as I thought about how shamelessly he'd stood in front of me when he'd left the pool. My mouth went dry as I thought about the water glistening off his skin and dripping off the long, thick cock swinging between his legs. He was so tall and broad that I shouldn't have been surprised that everything on him would be big, but it had still made my breath hitch in my chest and heat pool in my core.

"Get a grip, Sloane. He's just a guy."

A massive guy who was the warlord of a Vandar horde and who was holding me captive as he sought his violent revenge. So, not just a guy.

I shook off that thought and reminded myself that even though he was a renegade Vandar, he'd kept his word. He hadn't touched me while we'd eaten, or when we'd been in the bathing pool, aside from saving me from hypothermia.

My fingers were still warming up, although the burning sensation had passed, and I could now feel my feet. I glanced at the icy blue water in one of the wedges of the circular pool. What kind of sadists bathed in water that cold? I shivered even thinking about it.

"His package wouldn't be so impressive if he spent too much time in there," I said to myself, imagining what kind of shrinkage the icy water would cause. The Vandar might seem to be more resistant to cold—they did walk around in nothing but skirts made from strips of leather—but they weren't made of stone.

I remembered the expression on Raas Ronnan's face as he'd told me we had a deal. As tough and scary as he was, there had been a flicker of something behind his eyes as he'd looked at me—hurt, pain, regret? I wasn't sure, and it had been so fleeting I'd almost missed it, but the warlord wasn't devoid of emotion.

At least he'd agreed, no matter what turmoil was churning inside him. The warlord clearly had some anger issues he needed to work out regarding his plot for vengeance, but he'd been clearheaded enough to agree that anything happening between us was a bad idea. Sure, it hadn't been official, and we hadn't shaken on it—if Vandar even shook to seal deals—but he'd seemed honest when he'd said he had to find a Vandar mate.

"That rules me out," I said, curious when I experienced a twinge of irritation. I wasn't upset that the Vandar had eliminated me because I wasn't the right species, was I?

"You were hoping *not* to be mauled by him," I reminded myself. Still, a part of me didn't like being discarded so easily.

I stood and let the water cascade from me. "Now you're being ridiculous."

Since Ronnan had left his quarters, I was emboldened to step leisurely from the bathing pool. I let the cool air hit my skin and water drip on the cold floor as I grabbed a length of fabric from the long countertop. It wasn't hard and scratchy like the towels at the resistance barracks. Instead, this fabric was smooth and soft, and it glided across my skin as I dried myself.

The Vandar were a curious type of warrior. On one hand, they were violent and brutal, known for wielding ancient weapons and wearing battle garb. On the other hand, they ate well, had steaming baths, and dried themselves with silky fabrics. I was certain that not even the leader of the Valox had anything close to this level of luxury.

I padded to the main room with the fabric wrapped around my chest. I'd left my clothes in the bathroom, but I didn't want to get back into a dirty flight suit right away. Not when I was so clean. I knew I shouldn't be enjoying being a prisoner of the Vandar—correction, the Lost Vandar—but it had been so long since I'd had a real bath or worn anything but a dingy flight suit that I couldn't help wanting to enjoy it for a bit longer.

As I sat on the edge of the round bed, my shoulders slumped, and all the energy drained from my body. Maybe it was the shock of the cold followed by the intensity of the heat. Maybe it was the fact that I was the only resistance fighter who hadn't allowed herself to celebrate the victory over the empire and release the stress of the rebellion. I'd remained on high alert, continuing my searches and refusing to accept that the Zagrath threat was eliminated. Maybe it was the strain of grief I'd never allowed myself to fully process. Whatever the reason, I was suddenly hit by a wave of exhaustion so powerful I could barely keep my eyes open.

I blinked slowly, my lids lingering before I forced them open again. I should not fall asleep. Not when I should be figuring out a way to escape and warn the Vandar. I slid my sluggish gaze to the door. On the other hand, I wasn't going anywhere with the guards posted outside, and I'd already determined that the Raas' quarters held no way of escape.

I stifled a yawn, and my eyes watered. It wouldn't hurt if I rested my eyes for a little while, would it? I reclined on the bed, sighing as I sank into the softness. Again, the Vandar raiders surprised me. Raas Ronnan's bed wasn't some kind of hard, torturous warrior's bed that would keep him on high alert while he slept. It was pillowy soft, and the dark covers were as buttery as the cloth wrapped around me.

"Just a short nap," I mumbled as I tugged back the covers and wiggled underneath.

My mind drifted to the thought of the massive Vandar sleeping in bed next to me. Would he sleep in his battle kilt, or did the Vandar have special clothes for sleeping? Somehow I doubted either was the case. Raas Ronnan would sleep naked, just like I was doing, with the silky sheets caressing my skin. I was sure of it. What would I do if he insisted on sleeping naked with me? My pulse quickened even as the questions drifted away like the tendrils of a fading dream and I fell into a deep sleep.

CHAPTER
SIXTEEN

Ronnan

Droplets of water trailed down my back as I thundered through the warbird, leaping from one steel platform to another, and bounding up staircases as they rattled beneath my thick boots. Raiders moved aside after snapping their heels together in salute as I passed, gaining them growls of acknowledgment.

The cold air was brisk on my skin after the warm steam of the bathing chamber, but my skin still buzzed from touching the female. Sloane, I reminded myself. Her name was Sloane. And I hadn't merely touched her. I'd held her in my arms.

I closed my eyes for a beat outside the command deck, forcing images of the human female—and her perfect naked body—from my mind. I was the Raas of my horde. I could not afford to be distracted by a female who could never be anything more than a pawn in my plan for revenge.

A guttural sound of disgust slipped from my lips as I remembered the deal Sloane claimed we'd made. What had I foolishly promised? Not to take her as a mate? That would not be hard to do. I'd claimed many females without taking them as a true mate. Every pleasurer who'd warmed my bed had done so with the understanding that she could never be my mate. Sloane would be no different.

If she'd intended for her deal to keep me from her entirely, the female was very mistaken. I might have no desire to claim what wasn't freely given, but that didn't mean I didn't intend for her to succumb to me. She was living in my quarters, after all. She was my captive. In all ways that mattered to Vandar rules of war, she was mine.

My heart swelled at this thought, even as unease tickled the back of my brain. She could not be mine for good. Only until she'd served her purpose. Then I would have to release her so I could take a Vandar female as my true mate.

I touched a hand to the dark marks curling across my chest. Only union with my true mate would prompt my mating marks to extend down my arms and stomach and cause them to appear on her skin as well. It didn't matter that the human mates taken by the other Vandar had also taken their marks. It was different for me. I needed to fulfill the path set out for me and choose a Vandar mate. Then the destiny set for me by my father would be complete, and I would have vindicated my lineage.

I blew out a breath, trying to dislodge the weight that settled on my chest whenever I thought of my destiny and duty, the two entwined as one. It would not be long until I led my horde to victory, so we could complete our mission and realize our true purpose. No longer would we be lost.

Squaring my shoulders, I strode through the wide, arched doors that slid apart and onto my command deck. "Report!"

Kaiven pivoted from his standing console to face me. "We are monitoring space for any transmissions or signatures that might reveal Vandar warbirds using invisibility shielding."

I took my position on the platform above the warriors at their posts and braced my hands on my hips, the skin on my waist still damp. The view from the wide stretch of glass had not changed noticeably since I'd left. "Nothing?"

My battle chief shook his head with a frown. "Nothing of consequence."

"We have intercepted chatter about a missing pilot." Ayden joined me by jumping up and standing by my side, our shoulders brushing as he also faced the view screen. He handed me my battle axe, which I hooked onto my belt as I inclined my head at him in silent thanks. "It would seem the female told us the truth about who she is."

"She has not lied to me."

Kaiven folded his arms over his chest. "Yet. You cannot trust females, Raas."

"If she'd been lying, the truth would have slipped out while she was under the influence of the fire water," I told him.

Kaiven's eyebrows popped up, and my *majak* swiveled his head to look at me, although he made no comment.

"Do you trust me, Kaiven?" I asked, impatience flaring within me. My battle chief was responsible for advising me on strategy regarding war, not females.

He thrust out his chest. "Of course, Raas."

"Then trust me when I tell you that the female is no threat to us, nor has she attempted to deceive us. She is who she claims to be, which makes her valuable cargo and a useful pawn." I drummed my fingers on the carved hilt of my axe as I slid my gaze to my communications chief. "Now tell me about the intercepted chatter about a missing pilot."

"Nothing specific, Raas," he said, gripping both sides of his black console as he studied the readouts. "No call signs or coordinates, but several ships are searching the sector for a pilot."

I rocked back on my heels. That tracked with a rebel force searching for a missing pilot. "How far are we from the searching ships?"

The raider tilted his head to meet my eyes. "They have been flying near enough that they might have crashed into one of our horde ships if we hadn't steered around them."

"No indication they have detected us then?"

"No, Raas."

I smiled. That meant the Vandar had not revealed the secrets of our invisibility shielding to their allies. I was not surprised by this. It was one thing to fight with someone. It was another to share secrets that had kept the Vandar safe for generations. If the information slipped into the wrong hands, it would mean the end of the Vandar hordes flying unseen across space. The empire might have been defeated, but that did not change who the Vandar had become over generations of living in the shadows.

"Send a transmission in response," I said.

"Raas?" My communications chief blinked at me as if he'd misheard me.

"I wish to respond to these searching ships and tell them that they do not need to worry about their missing pilot."

"But Raas," Ayden dropped his voice to a conspiratorial hush. "Sending a transmission will give them the ability to triangulate our location. Our presence will no longer be a secret."

"They still will be unable to detect our precise location or see us, but our mission is not to enter Vandar territory and remain invisible."

My *majak* nodded, understanding dawning on him. "You wish to draw out the Vandar by alerting their allies of our presence."

I gave him a slight nod. "I wish to tell the Valox that their pilot is alive and well." And naked in my quarters, I thought with some amount of pleasure. I pinned my communications chief with an intent look. "Send the transmission."

He clicked his heels and tapped his fingers rapidly across his smooth console. "It is done."

Then I cut my gaze to my battle chief. "Reposition us and ready the horde to assume the amoeba formation."

"Yes, Raas." He also busied himself at his console, the engines rumbling as thrusters moved us from our previous position.

Then the command deck went quiet as we all waited for what we knew was inevitable. We didn't have to wait long. Soon, one ship appeared on our screen, just as gray and battle worn as the fighter Sloane had been flying. Then another. Like Ayden had predicted, they'd been able to find us from our transmission, but that didn't mean they knew where we were exactly—or who we were.

My communications chief spun to me, his kilt swinging. "Incoming hail."

"On screen," I ordered.

The view of space vanished, replaced by the startled faces of two females sitting in the cockpit of a ship. Their eyes widened as they took us in.

"What kind of Vandar are you?" One of the females finally said, which earned her a smack on the arm from the other.

"I am Raas Ronnan of the Kyrie Vandar. If you wish to see your pilot again, you will tell your Vandar friends that we have returned."

SEVENTEEN

Cassie peered at the console for the hundredth time since she and Thea had sent their last transmission. "Maybe this wasn't such a great idea."

They'd been flying in a search pattern near Sloane's recovered ship along with several other Valox fighters and hadn't found a trace of where their friend could have gone or tracked any other ships in the area.

Thea glanced at her, one eyebrow cocked. "Searching for Sloane?"

"No. *Us* piloting this ship and leading this mission. You're an engineer and I'm a navigator. Neither of us are pilots or experts at search and rescue missions."

Thea frowned. "First of all, we both can pilot a transport like this. It's not combat flying. And who better to look for Sloane than the people who know her best?"

Cassie worked her bottom lip between her teeth. "What good does knowing her do? They found her ship empty with no signs of struggle or a battle. So what if we know what type of music she likes, and her favorite food? You and I both know that she'd never leave her post willingly, which means something bad happened."

Thea put a hand on her friend's shoulder. "We also know Sloane is tough, and incredibly stubborn. As long as her ship was intact, that means she is, too. And we're going to find her."

Cassie nodded but didn't look confident. "What if she found what she was looking for? What if the Zagrath are still out there? If they find her and discover she's part of the resistance…" Her words drifted off as something flashed across her screen. "We're getting a transmission."

Thea wasted no time reading it. "It says we don't need to worry about our missing pilot. She's safe."

Cassie slapped her hand against the smooth console. "That's it? Who sent this?"

Thea's finger danced across the screen. "I can't tell, but I can figure out the part of space from where it originated."

"It's close." Cassie's heart pounded. "Setting a course to the coordinates now and sending them to the other ships."

"Punching it," Thea said, pushing the ship as fast as it could go.

Cassie glanced at her friend beside her, noticing that the usually cool and collected engineer was jiggling her leg and fiddling with the end of her long braid. She was more worried than she was letting on, a fact Cassie wasn't sure made her feel better or worse.

After flying for a while, Thea sat up straighter. "We're here."

Cassie peered out the front of the ship. "Are you sure? There's nothing out there."

"Nothing we can see." Thea frowned as she tapped on her console. "I'm sending a hail in case whoever took her is still nearby and just out of visual range." After a beat, she jerked back. "We got a response. Incoming hail."

The flat screen between their two consoles flickered to life. Two males with platinum hair and bare chests filled the screen, leather straps crossing their shoulders and black ink marking their exposed skin.

"What kind of Vandar are you?" Thea asked, and Cassie instinctively smacked her arm.

One of the males inclined his head slightly. "I am Raas Ronnan of the Kyrie Vandar. If you wish to see your pilot again, you will tell your Vandar friends that we have returned."

Cassie shot Thea a look and whispered, "Kyrie Vandar? What is that?"

Thea twitched one shoulder, looking back to the screen quickly. "You admit that you took our pilot?"

"She was in Vandar space. Her ship was disabled. We found her. She is now a guest of our horde."

Both women glanced again at the empty space. But now they knew they were most likely surrounded by an invisible horde of Vandar warbirds.

"A guest?" Cassie blurted out without thinking. "Then she's not a prisoner?"

The Raas smiled slowly. "We will happily return her to you once you have brought a Vandar horde to us."

"A Vandar horde? How would we be able to bring you a Vandar horde?" Cassie waved a hand at him. "Aren't you Vandar?"

Thea put a calming hand on Cassie's leg without taking her eyes off the screen. "If we do this, you'll release our pilot?"

The Raas hesitated before nodding.

"How do we know you really have her?" Thea asked. "How do we know she's still alive?"

Cassie drew in a sharp breath. It hadn't occurred to her that Sloane could have been taken and killed.

The Vandar warlord's smile slipped. "Sloane is alive, I promise you."

Thea's leg stopped jiggling when he uttered her friend's name.

"You are her friends, aren't you?" He continued, glancing from one to the other. "You are Cassie and Thea."

Cassie made a small squeaking sound.

"She has told me about you." The Raas shifted from one leg to the other. "If you wish to be reunited with her, find a Vandar horde and bring them here. Tell them that the Kyrie Vandar have returned."

"What—?" Cassie started to say before the Raas flicked a hand in the air and the transmission ended.

Thea expelled a loud breath. "Well, we found her."

Cassie slumped in her seat. "But we can't get her back unless we track down a Vandar horde. It's not like we have an open channel to them."

The Vandar and Valox might have teamed up to fight the empire, but the Vandar remained secretive and shadowy warriors who held the locations of their colonies and hordes close to the chest.

"I have a contact." Thea busily tapped new coordinates into the navigational system.

Cassie gaped at her. "You know a Vandar?"

"I met one of their Raisas when I was liberating a planet." Her knee began to jiggle again. "Let's hope Tara remembers me—and that Raas Kaalek is willing to meet with these Kyrie Vandar."

Cassie almost groaned out loud. She'd heard a bit about Raas Kaalek, and willingness was not one of the words used to describe the notoriously impulsive and deadly raider.

EIGHTEEN

Ronnan

I left the command deck with my heart pounding as loud as my boots as I made my way through the cavernous warbird, the steel stairs and suspended walkways rattling and shaking beneath my merciless stomping. We were one step closer to facing off against the Vandar. One step closer to exacting our revenge on the descendants of those who'd wronged our fathers.

Fire coursed through my veins as I imagined laying eyes on the Vandar for the first time. Since our exile, we'd never seen any of our species, except our own sires. There were none in our horde of Vandar-Selkee raiders who shared the inky-black hair of the original Vandar, although we shared many of their other characteristics. Like them, we carried mating marks on our skin, and we'd inherited the Vandar build and long tails. But unlike them, we were the exiled.

I growled. The sound was swallowed up by the echoing shouts and rumbles that spiraled up from the warbird's web of walkways and twisting staircases below. The Kyrie Vandar had been on the hunt for vengeance for so long that it almost seemed unreal that it was within our grasp—and all because we'd happened upon a human female stranded in space.

My thoughts went to Sloane as I approached my quarters. When I'd left her, I'd told her she had a deal. But what had I agreed to? That I wouldn't take her as a mate? There was no question that I could never do that. My pulse quickened as my mind twisted the promise, molding it to the desires coursing through me like a fever.

I made no promise that I would not claim her. Even now, memories of her naked body made my cock ache. I held my arms in front of me to keep it from tenting my kilt as I staggered the last few steps to my quarters. The warriors flanking the arched steel door clicked their heels in salute as I passed and entered the room, slowing my step when I was met with a hush that was in stark contrast to the constant clatter and buzz outside.

For the briefest moment, I thought she was gone. There was no sound of splashing in the bathing chamber. There was no movement anywhere. Then my gaze rested on the bed and the lump beneath the covers.

I removed my boots so I could approach with more stealth, and I unhooked my battle axe and hung it on the stand near the door. She was feisty enough that I didn't trust her anywhere near a weapon.

As I drew closer to the round bed, I spotted a pile of dark fabric to one side. I swung my head to the doorway leading to the bathing chamber and my heart tripped in my chest. Her clothes still remained on the floor next to the bathing pool, which meant she was naked in my bed.

It was Vandar custom to sleep unclothed, but I'd learned that many species wore special outfits to their beds. As odd as I'd found this habit, it no longer surprised me. It did surprise me that humans would also sleep naked.

My fingers tingled with the urge to pull back the covers, but I remained standing beside her, looking down as she slept on her stomach, her damp hair splayed across her back and her head resting on her folded hands. I gently brushed a wet strand of hair off one shoulder, holding my breath to see if she would react to my touch.

She released a breathy sigh and rolled over, the dark fabric slipping so that her breasts were barely covered. It would only take a single hard snatch to rip the covers off her and expose her fully and then another quick movement to pin her body beneath mine.

I grunted brusquely. I did not want her that way, although I could easily take her. I wanted her to want me. To beg for me. To cry out my name in pleasure, not in fear.

I knew all too well how to incite terror. From her, I wanted something no battle or conquest could give me.

I leaned down so that my face was next to hers, our cheeks brushing as I inhaled the scent of the fire water she carried on her skin. My cock throbbed with the need to touch more than her cheek, but I forced myself to resist the primal and brutal urges that had defined me for so long.

"Sloane," I husked.

With a moan, she looped her arms around my neck and pulled me down to her. Although her action wasn't harsh, it was so surprising that I did stumble forward, catching myself from crushing her at the last moment. I braced myself on my elbows above her as she slid her arms down my back, her fingers warm on my flesh.

"Come to bed," she whispered. "I've been waiting for you."

Her eyes were closed, and her voice was dreamy. As much as I wished to fall into bed beside the female and lose myself in the sweet touch of her, I feared it wasn't me she was beckoning to her bed. Jealousy surged through me, but then I remembered that I should not covet what would never be mine. She would never fall for me, and I would never take her as a mate. That had been the deal.

Then she slid one hand up into my hair and yanked my mouth to hers. Hunger jackknifed through me as she kissed me, her lips opening so my tongue could tangle with hers.

All deals were off.

CHAPTER
NINETEEN

Sloane

M y thoughts were a muddled swirl as they danced in my head, balancing me on the precipice between the waking world and sleep. I was both groggy and acutely aware of the touch of the soft sheets and the cool of the air. I rolled over and sighed, memories of the Vandar warlord wet and dripping tormenting me and teasing me. Why couldn't I rid my mind of him, and drift fully into sleep? Why did visions of the frightening raider insist on crowding my mind and chasing away any chance of peaceful rest?

I should have been thinking about Leo—or anyone else but the Vandar who was holding me in his quarters as his captive. But it was the massive alien with alabaster hair and a long tail who consumed me and made heat throb traitorously between my legs.

"Sloane." The velvety deep voice sent frissons of unwanted desire ricocheting through me.

I instinctively raised my arms, hooking them around a neck and pulling the voice closer to me. I needed more of that hunger that was so evident when he'd said my name. Sliding my hands down the warm, bare flesh made me realize what I wanted.

"Come to bed," I whispered. "I've been waiting for you."

I was barely aware of the words before they tumbled from my lips. They barely sounded like mine they were so high and breathy. Had I ever sounded like that before? Had I ever beckoned someone to come to bed with me?

Without opening my eyes, I could feel the heat of his body above mine and the thundering of his heartbeat. His quick breath feathered my ear, but it wasn't enough. I needed more. I slid one hand up into his long hair and yanked his mouth to mine.

Instantly, his lips parted mine and his tongue tangled with mine. I was snapped from my haze, awareness returning me to the waking world. For a moment, I allowed myself to get lost in the taste of him. His kiss was so claiming and so intoxicating that I felt myself slipping under his spell again.

Then I pressed my hands against his chest and pushed hard against him, tearing my mouth from his and panting. This was no dream and the man I'd imagined was no fantasy.

Ronnan was on top of me, his body between my splayed legs and his chest brushing my hard nipples that were no longer covered. His eyes were molten with unbridled lust and his breathing was ragged.

"What are you doing?" I spluttered as I attempted to wriggle under the weight of him. "Get off me!"

He tilted his head at me. "You are the one who touched me. You are the one who invited me to your bed. You are the one who kissed me."

My jaw dropped, but I stopped on the verge of calling him a liar. I *had* told him to come to bed. I *had* pulled his mouth to mine.

Raas Ronnan sat back, shifting so that he was straddling my waist but not resting his full weight on me. Still, I was immobilized under him.

"I didn't know what I was saying. I didn't know it was you."

His eyes flashed—amusement or anger, I couldn't tell which. "Who did you think you were inviting into my bed if not for me?"

I huffed out a frustrated breath. Who had I thought he was? I didn't want to think about that or admit that it might have been him rolling around in my fantasies.

He leaned down and I jutted out a hand to slap him, more of a knee-jerk reaction to defend myself than an attempt to inflict damage. As if I could.

He caught my hand with reflexes so cat-like I sucked in a quick breath.

"You should not strike a Raas in his own bed," he growled. "You will lose."

His arrogant words irritated me, even though they were undeniably true. I scowled at him and tried to buck him off me, but the brute barely moved. I lashed out with my other hand, and he deftly caught that one, as well. He held both of my wrists in his hands while I wiggled beneath him.

I was suddenly aware that my breasts were bare and quivering with each of my jerky movements. He seemed to become aware of this too, his gaze sliding slowly down my body. He twisted his head to one side as if trying to restrain himself then pinned me with a carnal look.

"You don't want to fight me," he practically purred as he pinned my hands over my head and wrapped his tail around my legs to hold them in place.

"Really?" I gritted out. "You could have fooled me."

A low chuckle shook his body as he brushed his lips across my forehead in a surprisingly gentle kiss. "Do you want me to stop this? And do not lie to me. I do not tolerate lies, Sloane."

My body trembled, desire overtaking any fear I might have felt as the alien kissed both my eyelids and then my cheeks.

"Tell me to stop if you wish it." The deep timbre of his voice slid through my bones and unfurled a sinful heat between my legs.

I could only whimper in response as he lifted his head. His gaze was pure fire.

CHAPTER
TWENTY

Ronnan

It was excruciating torture to be so close to her and only whisper my lips over her skin, but I would only have her if she gave herself willingly. She would beg for me to take her. Not to stop.

Any brute could force a female smaller than himself. I was not just anyone. I was a Raas of the Vandar, the leader of the Kyrie Vandar who had crossed galaxies to claim what was rightfully mine. I would not have to take this by force.

"Tell me to stop if you wish it." I pinned her gaze with my own as my heart slammed against my ribs, needing her to beckon me with her eyes and her silky sighs.

Her lashes fluttered as she bit her bottom lip. Was she afraid she would stop me? Was her rational mind at war with her body?

"This does not break our deal," I told her as I fought to tear my gaze from her tempting lips.

She loosed a breath and a mangled attempt at a laugh. "No?"

I shook my head. "Our agreement still stands, but that does not mean we cannot live in the moment and enjoy the pleasures of the flesh."

"So, this is just sex?"

My shoulder muscles went taut. I wasn't used to females who were not paid for their affections being so direct. Maybe there was an advantage to being with a fighter like myself who understood that every day and every battle could be your last.

I eyed the pulse thrumming at her neck. "If that is what you want." I lowered my head to kiss the soft skin that betrayed her emotions. "What do you want?"

Sloane gasped as my tongue traced a meandering line to the hollow of her throat. "I want..."

I readjusted my grip on her wrists and tightened the grasp of my tail. "Remember, I will know if you lie, and I will punish you for it."

"Punish me?" Her voice cracked.

"The Vandar do not tolerate lies. Not within our ranks, or from our prisoners of war. I demand nothing from you but the truth." I circled the tip of my tongue in the silky divot of her throat. "I will not make you spread your legs for me, but if that is your desire, you *will* tell me." A sharp stab of carnal hunger twisted my gut. "And you will tell me everything you want me to do to you."

Her breath quickened, and she squirmed in my grasp. My cock ached as it pressed against my kilt and her warm body.

"If you won't tell me what you want, then you will have to tell me what you don't." I continued kissing down her chest, capturing one peaked nipple and being rewarded by her arching her back into me. I sucked and swirled my tongue around the pebbled skin, moving my attentions from one tight peak to the other, until she was moaning.

I released her nipple and looked up. "Tell me to stop, Sloane."

She met my gaze across the curves of her body, her eyes pools of molten heat, but she didn't speak.

I let out a snarl as I released her wrists and reluctantly uncoiled my tail. I moved down her body, pulling the covers entirely off her and spreading her legs so I could settle my body between them. She sat up and watched me, the look in her gaze one of both torment and hunger.

"This is where human females have their pleasure center, is it not?" I'd heard rumors of the bundle of nerves that could make human women scream with pleasure without even entering them.

She nibbled on her bottom lip. "I thought you'd never been with a human before."

"I have not, but talk of your little pleasure nubs has spread far and wide, thanks, I believe, to the Vandar here. Even pleasure houses in distant sectors now brag of having human pleasurers."

I slid a finger through her slickness, my own groan mingling with hers. "So wet for me."

"Before you ask," she said. "I don't want you to stop."

"I wasn't going to ask," I snarled, "Open your legs wider for me."

She sucked in a breath, muttering something about me being an arrogant ass.

"Are you going to do what I tell you to or are you going to disobey me?" I husked.

Her legs fell open as she released a needy sigh. I almost wished she'd chosen to disobey me, but there was no doubt in mind she would challenge me in the future. I was counting on it.

I set my mouth on her as she dropped her head back and let her legs fall open. The taste of her was intoxicating and like nothing I'd ever experienced. As hard as my cock was, I had no urge to hurry as I lapped at her sweet juices.

I dragged my tongue through her hot flesh until I found a slick bundle that made her jerk when I circled it with my tongue. Satisfaction pulsed through me as I worked it gently, the sounds of her ragged breath and needy moans guiding me to go faster or slower. Her body writhed beneath me, and as she began to tremble, I slid a thick finger inside her warmth.

"Ronnan!" Sloane raked her fingers through my hair, tangling them and holding my head to her as her movements became less controlled. Breathy, keening noises escaped her lips while I added another finger to her tightness and slowly dragged them in and out.

Hearing her gasp my name sent desire through me like shock-waves. To my raiders, I was Raas. Only my *majak* occasionally addressed me as Ronnan, and never with the raw need that clung to Sloane's voice as she cried out my name.

Suddenly, there was nothing I wanted more than to hear her say my name again, desperate and hungry for the pleasure I was giving her. I needed to hear my name on her lips like I needed air to breathe.

I sucked her slick nub and moved my fingers faster, curving them up to stroke her inner walls. With a scream, she bucked against me, her body clenching around my fingers like a vise. She spasmed and dug her fingers into my hair, her thighs clenching around my head until she finally flopped back on the bed, her body sagging and her fingers slipping from my head.

I gave a satisfied growl, sliding my fingers from her and kissing the inside of her tender thighs as her chest hitched in uneven breaths. I licked my lips, savoring the sweetness of her, but knowing I needed more.

I moved my way up her body until I was staring into her half-lidded eyes. "Are you ready to scream my name again?"

CHAPTER
TWENTY-ONE

Sloane

I blinked languidly at Ronnan, my body humming with the glow of an incredible orgasm. One that had been given to me by an alien with a very talented tongue. My pulse was already racing, or it would have quickened at the thought.

"I'm ready for more," I said, hooking one leg around him.

He gave me an arch smile. "More of my mouth?"

My pussy clenched at this, but I shook my head. As amazing as that had been, I wanted him inside me. I needed it.

"Tell me what you want." He kissed me softly and slowly. More gently than I'd ever imagined a Vandar warlord could be.

I put both of my hands on the sides of his face and held his gaze captive. "I want you to fuck me like you own me. Like I belong to you."

As soon as the words slipped from my lips, my face burned. What the hell was that? I spend my life being fiercely independent and proving that I don't need anyone and the moment I'm with an alien, I tell him to dominate me. Seriously, Sloane?

His smile widened even as his eyes flashed dangerously. "I don't have to pretend. You do belong to me. Your ship was in Vandar space. By our raiding laws, your vessel and all the contents—including you—belong to my horde and to me." He cut his gaze to the door. "I have guards at the door to keep you from leaving my quarters. You don't think I'm ever letting you go now, do you? After I've tasted you and felt you come on my tongue? And now that I'm going to fuck you until you beg me for mercy?"

My breath caught in my throat. I didn't know if this was dirty talk or if he was being serious, but his forceful words made heat pulse between my legs.

The Raas cupped my chin in one hand. "Tell me that you understand you're mine now. Tell me you belong to me and only me."

My mouth went dry and, the words stuck in my throat. Was this a game, or were we playing for real?

His grip on my jaw tightened as he shifted his weight and notched the broad crown of his cock at my opening. "Tell me."

I was almost panting with desire. My release had only made me desperate for more of him and more escape into the euphoric daze he'd put me under, which was fading.

"I'm yours," I said. "Only yours."

He growled, his lips stretching as if he was baring his teeth as the crown of his cock teased me. "You need this cock, don't you?"

I only moaned in response, twitching my hips toward him.

"You need to be fucked, to be tamed..." He pushed the head of his cock inside me, stretching me with his girth. "To submit." He kissed me again, this time hard and claiming, his tongue parting my lips and delving deep. As he ravished my mouth, he drove the rest of his rigid length into me.

When he'd filled me, he tore his lips from mine and held himself in place. I snatched needy breaths as my body adjusted to the size of him.

His gaze was on me, his brow furrowed and his own chest rising and falling quickly. He lowered his face until our foreheads touched. "You take me like you were made for me. How could a human be so perfect for a Vandar?"

It was a question he didn't wait for me to answer as he started to move inside me with slow, steady strokes. I wrapped my legs around him to pull him deeper and put my hands on his shoulders.

"Maybe my Vandar brothers knew something I did not when they took humans as mates," he whispered as he buried his face in my neck and nipped at the tender skin there. "If all human females feel like you do, I no longer wonder why they claimed them and made them their mates."

He didn't wait for a response from me before rolling me over quickly so that he was on his back and I was on top, my legs straddling his waist. I gasped from the even deeper angle as I was impaled his cock, but he grasped my hips and started to move me up and down his length.

I fell forward, catching myself and bracing my hands on his chest. His skin was slick with sweat, the black marks curling across his flesh as shiny as if they were painted.

"*Tvek*," he gritted out. "You look like a goddess riding me."

"You look like an alien warlord who gets what he wants."

His brows twitched, and his dark eyes sparkled. "Since I possess a beautiful female to fuck as much as I want, I do have what I want."

"You think you have me?" I teased him as I leaned forward and let my breasts brush his chest.

"I know I do."

I shook my head. "Arrogant."

A challenge glinted in his gaze as he used his grip on my hips to tilt my hips forward and pull his cock out, Before I could protest, something else was pushing inside me. I twisted my head with a gasp as I glanced behind me to see the tip of his tail disappearing inside me. The sensation of the furry tip stroking in and out was intense, but it seemed so scandalous and wrong that I groaned and dug my fingernails into the Vandar's chest.

"You like being fucked by my tail, don't you?"

I could only roll my head back and nod, which coaxed a moan from Ronnan as he slid his tail from me. I didn't have time to whimper my complaint before he had me on my hands and knees and was pressing my head into the soft surface of the bed as he thrust his cock into me from behind.

The Raas snatched my hands together and held them at the small of my back as he drove into me with a ferocity that made me cry out. "I know I have you, and I have no intention of letting you go." He curled his tail around so that it worked my clit as he pounded into me, and within moments, my body was shuddering as waves of pleasure swept over me. He threw back his head as he roared and pulsed hot into me, finally slumping forward and whispering into the nape of my neck. "Ever."

TWENTY-TWO

Ronnan

I rolled the game piece between my fingers silently, stealing a glance at Sloane sleeping on the bed. The red wood cylinder warmed the more I touched it, a product of the vindin tree it was crafted from, and I stopped before I caused it to spark and set the entire Zindar board on fire.

Usually, the Selkee game of strategy calmed my mind, but I found my thoughts wandering from the three-dimensional structure and the game pieces perched upon it. I spun the circular base to get a better view of the transparent platforms that were stacked in an asymmetrical spiral twisting up to a square large enough for a single, solitary cylinder. The winning piece.

At the moment, I was far from the top, even though I was playing against myself. I blew out a breath and reached for the goblet of Vandar wine I'd poured for myself.

"*Tvek*," I muttered before taking a sip. "You should be warming yourself in bed with the female." Then I corrected myself. "Sloane."

I let my gaze drift over to my bed again before giving my head a vigorous shake and tossing back the rest of my wine. I'd already allowed myself to slip once. I could not allow any more weakness.

I straightened and set my goblet on the long table, turning my attention back to the game. Zindar had helped me through many difficult times, and I was sure it would get me through this. It took a sharp mind to win the game, and I'd honed my skills over many hours—first against my mother, who'd taught me and my brother the traditional Selkee game, and then against Ayden, who was an even match for my playing.

My father had never bothered with the game. He'd embraced precious little about the Selkee world he'd been forced to inhabit—except my mother—and remained devoted to Vandar ways until the end. It was my father's voice I now heard ringing in my head and muddling my focus.

He'd drilled in me the need to avenge the wrongs perpetrated against him and his fellow Vandar exiles. As they'd forged the warbirds that would make up the hordes that we now flew toward our destiny, they'd made sure we knew what was expected of us. Find the Vandar. Claim our rightful place. Take Vandar mates. Restore our bloodline.

I grunted roughly. There had been nothing in that plan about falling for humans. It had never been something that had even approached the realm of possibility when we'd left on our mission. It was unthinkable.

My mind filled with thoughts of the human writhing beneath me, her moans and cries as hungry as mine. From the first taste of her, I'd been consumed with a familiarity that should have been impossible. There was no way a Raas of the Vandar—a Kyrie Raas who'd been raised far from where humans inhabited—should feel any connection to a woman like Sloane.

I frowned as I moved my game piece up a level and slotted it into a space, watching as the platforms shifted and moved accordingly. I lifted my palm to slam it on the table as I realized my tactical error, but I stopped myself before I struck the glossy surface.

I did not want to wake her from her sleep. Instead, I curled my hand into a fist and clenched my teeth as I reassessed the board and how many moves it would take me to salvage my foolishness.

I pushed back and slumped into my chair, scraping a hand through my hair. It was no use. What was done couldn't be undone—in Zindar and in life. I'd opened myself to Sloane the moment I'd allowed her to become more to me than leverage, and that had been a mistake.

It didn't matter how intoxicating I found her or how right it felt being with her. I could not take her as my mate and Raisa. It would ruin everything I'd worked for and unravel all of my father's plans. It didn't matter if we were reinstated to our rightful place among the Vandar if we didn't restore our bloodlines. A half-Selkee Raas could not take a human as his true mate and expect to return the Vandar empire to glory.

I lifted a hand to my chest and traced my fingers across my markings. I knew where they were by heart, and I also knew that when I found my true mate—my true Vandar mate—she would also take on my markings. It would link us forever in the Vandar mating bond. I could not be sure that would happen with a human, since I was only half Vandar. I could not risk taking a human mate like the other Vandar had. Not and achieve what was my destiny. No, the stubborn rebel fighter pilot would never be a Raisa of the Vandar.

Bile teased the back of my throat, but I choked it down. I allowed my gaze to shift to where Sloane's hair spilled across the pillow, and my cock ached as I thought back to being buried inside her and the heady sensation that I was complete for the first time in my life. I wanted that feeling again so much I had to grip the arms of the chair not to leap from it and run to the bed.

"It is impossible," I whispered darkly to myself as I looked away. I steadied my breath as my heart raced. I would have to give her up, turn her over to her friends in the Valox resistance, watch her walk away from me. There was no other way to fulfill the fate set for me by my father.

I jerked upright and glared at the Zindar board. Maybe it wouldn't be so hard, I told myself. It was probably the after-glow of sex that was making me think this was more than it was. Hadn't I bedded enough females and left them behind? This one would be no different.

I scowled at the game board, trying to harness all my focus as I drummed my fingers on the table.

"I take it you're not winning?"

I spun my head at the sound of her voice. Sloane had padded silently across the room with the gray sheets wrapped around her and her hair tousled. She eyed the Zindar board.

My heart lurched in my chest at the sight of her, and I emitted a low growl. "No, I'm not."

CHAPTER
TWENTY-THREE

Sloane

T'd woken and stretched like a cat. If I could have purred like one, I would have. I hadn't slept so well in as long as I could remember, and it was the first time in forever I'd actually felt rested.

Having your brains fucked out helped. I'd collapsed in a heap after Ronnan had come in me, and I'd even fallen asleep with him curled around my back and still inside me. I smiled thinking about how perfect he'd felt cocooning me, his huge body tucking around my smaller one. Then I'd rolled over, missing the warmth of him. He wasn't there.

For the span of a heartbeat, I'd panicked and wondered if I'd imagined it or maybe even dreamed it. Then I'd seen him at the long table staring at a contraption that appeared to be hovering in mid-air with finger-sized cylinders arranged on multiple transparent platforms.

I'd swung my legs to the floor, ignoring the shock of the cold on my bare feet, and tugged the sheet with me as I'd walked quietly toward him. Ronnan was also barefoot, wearing only a kilt. But not the leather one I'd seen before. This one was made of a nubby woven fabric, and it hung low on his waist. His face was set in a frown as he appraised what must have been some kind of game.

"I take it you're not winning?" I asked once I was closer.

He swung his head to me, his eyes widening as he took me in. Then a low growl rumbled from his chest. "No, I'm not."

I slid my gaze to the unusual structure on the table. "Is this a one-person game, or can I join you?"

He dragged a hand across the scruff on his cheeks. "You know how to play Zindar?"

"Zindar?" I shook my head. "Never heard of it, but I like games."

He gave me an arrogant grin. "Zindar is more than a game. It is a test of strategy and patience."

I wrapped the sheet more snugly around my chest and took the chair closest to him and the game. "Perfect. I love games of strategy. What are the rules?"

The Vandar cocked his head at me. "You wish to challenge me in Zindar? I have played this game since I was a boy."

I shrugged. "Then I'll lose." I gave him a confident smile of my own. "Or not. I'm a fast learner. Now are you going to teach me or what?"

He shook his head as if he was reluctantly giving in to my request, but I could see the smile quirking the corners of his lips. He cleared the multilevel board of all the pieces and then arranged them on the bottom squares as he explained the rules. I listened carefully as he outlined the objective of the game and how to move the wooden cylinders, how the rules changed according to the level, and how each move of the pieces shifted the layout of the board.

"So, the board changes each time I move a piece?" I clarified.

He didn't answer with words, instead plucking one of the pieces and slotting it into a space. The board clamped around the wooden cylinder before the platforms rotated, split, and twisted into a new configuration.

I scrunched my lips to one side, my pulse fluttering. "You have to readjust your game plan after each move because the board becomes entirely different."

He grunted. "You still wish to play me?"

I rubbed my hands together. "Definitely. This is like being in a battle in the sky that changes every second. You blast one ship from the sky, and then you have two others coming at you from the rear."

Ronnan reset the board and inclined his head at me. "Your move."

I nibbled the corner of my lip as I considered my opening move. "How have I never heard of this game before? I was sure I knew all the games of strategy."

"It is a Selkee game. As far as I know, it has not traveled beyond the planet's borders."

"Selkee is where you're from?" I moved my piece conservatively, glancing up at him. "I mean, after you left Vandar territory."

"Our fathers were the ones who left Vandar territory." The Raas didn't look up as he studied the board. "None in the new hordes know any home but Selk, the planet our fathers settled on after they were exiled."

"Your mothers are from Selk?"

He gave a brusque nod, moving his piece and watching as the board's new structure clicked into place. "The Kyrie Vandar are all half Selkee."

"I don't know anything about your home world, but they have impressive games."

He allowed himself a small smile. "The Selkee are known for their intellect. They do not have military might, but they are prized as great strategists and thinkers." The pride was evident in his voice. "My mother taught me Zindar to teach me to think strategically."

"She sounds smart." I carefully moved a second piece, frowning when the board shifted and relegated my first piece back to the bottom level.

Ronnan's smile faded. "She was."

I didn't comment on his use of the past tense, but it was clear his mother was no longer alive. I wondered how old he'd been when he'd lost her, but I didn't wish to stir up sad memories by asking him. "Was it only you and your parents?"

He shook his head. "I have a brother and sister, as well as a half-brother who is full Selkee."

"Busy house." I eyed the board then him. "Are any of them on this mission with you?"

Another shake of the head.

"Do you miss them?"

Ronnan grunted. "My family is complicated, but I do miss them. Some more than others."

"Sounds like a normal family to me. Will you ever see them again, or is this a one-way trip?"

He flicked his gaze to me after I moved a game piece. "Home is not far enough that we won't go back. Those left behind await our victorious return."

I studied the board as he hovered his hand over one of the polished wood cylinders. "So, your mother taught you strategy and your father taught you how to be a warrior?"

He moved one of his pieces and the board shifted once more, one piece landing on top of the other and being expelled from the board. He caught it before it rolled off the table.

"My mother did not believe in my father's plan for revenge. She believed it to be bad strategy."

I couldn't tell from his voice if he'd sided with his mother or father, but since he was leading a horde of raiders into Vandar territory, I guess that was my answer.

"What else did your mother believe?"

Ronnan rolled the discarded game piece between two fingers. "She did not believe in such a thing as half-bloods. She despised when my father used that term. If he wanted to provoke her, that was always a sure way."

"Your own father called you a half-blood?" I wasn't surprised his mother had been angry at this. My own skin prickled with heat at the thought of Ronnan's father being so cruel to his own son.

The Vandar met my eyes, but his were shuttered. "He respected the Selkee, but he believed in the purity of Vandar blood. Without a Vandar mate, there are no mating marks."

I remembered hearing something about Vandar mating marks, but I also knew I'd heard that the human mates had gotten them. "Your mother never got Vandar mating marks?"

Ronnan dropped his gaze to the board, giving his head a curt shake. "None of the Selkee did. My mother said it was because the Selkee descended from magical beings that they could not be marked by another. My father believed it proved that his son needed a Vandar mate. Only with a Vandar female could I be sure to restore our blood line."

He lifted his head and locked his gaze on me. I allowed the words to sink in before blinking a few times.

"Don't worry about me." I flapped my hands in front of me. "I told you I have no designs on becoming your queen or Raisa or whatever you call the wife of a Raas. You're a lot of fun in bed, but that doesn't change anything. I still need to get back to the resistance and my job, not to mention my friends."

Even as I said the words, regret twisted my gut. It was true that I wanted to return to my friends and my life, but Ronnan was more than just a bit of fun in bed. Even though we were complete opposites and came from different worlds, I'd felt a deeper connection to him than I had to anyone. Even Leo.

I pushed aside that traitorous thought and reminded myself of the deal. I couldn't fall for him—no matter what.

"I am glad to hear that," the Raas said. "And to know that I pleased you in bed."

My cheeks warmed as I returned my attention to the game, and I attempted to ignore his hot gaze on me. I spotted an opening on the board and moved my piece. The levels adjusted, and my piece was suddenly within striking distance of the top.

Ronnan made a gruff noise in the back of his throat. "Are you sure *you* do not possess Selkee blood?"

I took this to mean that I was winning, but before I could gloat properly, a beep sounded at the door to his quarters. Then the door swished open to reveal the warrior who'd escorted me through the ship, the one Ronnan called *majak*. He did not look pleased.

CHAPTER
TWENTY-FOUR

Ronnan

"I apologize for interrupting, Raas."

I brushed off my *majak's* apology as we strode through the ship. "You did not interrupt."

He glanced at me pointedly. I knew it was not lost on my most trusted advisor that I'd been in none of the gear I'd had when I'd left the command deck earlier. He'd waited for me to change back into my battle kilt and boots, handing me my battle axe as I'd joined him at the door.

"Does the human know Zindar?" He asked as we leapt from one suspended platform to another, the steel rattling beneath our heavy boots.

"I was teaching her."

Ayden grunted, but I could hear the questioning tone in the sound. "You still maintain that the prisoner is leverage, nothing more?"

"Nothing more." The words were bitter on my lips, but I didn't allow myself to dwell on them as we took a wide metal staircase two tall steps at a time and entered the command deck.

"Report," I called as I took my position overlooking the dark consoles and the Vandar raiders standing at them. "Have we heard from the Valox?"

Heels snapped together as my warriors saluted me.

"Not yet, Raas." My communications chief swiveled to face me, his expression tense. "No transmissions from Valox or Vandar."

I crossed my arms over my chest and nodded. I had not expected an instantaneous response, but the longer we went without communications, the greater the chance that there was a reason for the delay.

"We have detected movements of various ships on long-range scanners," my battle chief said, gripping the hilt of his battle axe as he joined me and Ayden on the platform.

I inclined my head to acknowledge Kaiven as he clicked his heels together. "What type of movements?"

"From what I can tell, they are assuming defensive positions around planets."

I growled. It was as I'd suspected. The Valox had warned others of our arrival, and the sector was bracing for a battle or attacks. I braced my legs wide and rested my hands on my hips. "It isn't wise to keep the horde here while our opponents ready for an attack."

"I agree, Raas." Kaiven exchanged a glance with my *majak*. "I recommend moving us to another location."

"Move the rest of the horde," I said. "Have them disperse and stay invisible. We will stay and wait for the Vandar."

My battle chief's brow furrowed. "One ship to take on another Vandar horde?"

"Our horde is fast," I reminded him. "They will come join the fight when we need them."

Ayden nodded. "The other Vandar might not be expecting us to have broken our horde. We could surround them."

I stared out the wide glass that overlooked space. The blackness was peaceful and empty, but I knew the dangers the sector held—and all that was hidden.

"You have your orders," I told Kaiven.

"It is done." He tapped his heels again before striding back to his console.

"Without our horde, we will not be able to confuse our enemy with our amoeba formation," Ayden said in a low voice.

"Our enemy invented the amoeba. It will not confuse them. Fighting our own kind means we will not have the same advantages."

"But we are not just like them," my *majak* said. "We have lived apart from the Vandar."

I thought of what I'd told Sloane about the Selkee. "And we were trained by great strategists who valued brains over brawn."

Ayden stifled a laugh. "Unlike our fathers."

Our fathers had been as close as we were and had been so similar in their manner and mindset that Ayden and I had lived nearly identical childhoods and grown up side-by-side. We'd been trained together and often punished together. Even closer had been our mothers, sisters who'd raised us to be brothers in every way. I'd been closer to Ayden than I had been to my own brother, for many reasons, and it was Ayden who was by my side now and who I considered a true brother.

Thinking of my Selkee mother brought my thoughts back to the Zindar board and the female waiting in my quarters to finish the game.

"I trust you, brother." I clamped a hand on my *majak's* shoulder. "You have command. When the Valox or Vandar arrive, summon me."

He gaped at me as I left the command deck as quickly as I'd entered it. I'd spoken the truth. I did trust Ayden. He was as much the leader of the horde as I was, and the Kyrie Vandar were in good hands with him at the helm. In the meantime, I had a game to win.

I thundered through the cavernous ship, pounding through suspected walkways that shook as I walked and jumping from platform to platform until I reached the guards flanking the door to my quarters. They tapped their heels as I passed between them and through the arched door that parted for me.

Once inside, I stopped. I'd expected to see Sloane sitting at the table, wrapped in her sheet waiting for me or maybe back in bed. Instead, she was dressed in the flight suit we'd found her in and sitting across from a Vandar warrior on the other side of the Zindar board.

She looked up when I entered, grinning at me. "That was fast."

The table was no longer empty save for the game. Domed plates and trays of food filled the center of the long surface, along with fresh carafes of wine.

The Vandar sitting across from Sloane leapt to his feet and spun around. "Apologies, Raas. I did not mean to stay so long."

"It's my fault," Sloane said. "He delivered food—I'm not sure if it's lunch or dinner, since I have no concept of time in here—and I asked him to give me some pointers on the game."

The Vandar lowered his head, his tail drooping. "I did not want to refuse her request." He glanced at me, his expression tortured.

I understood immediately that the raider didn't know if this female was a prisoner or a guest or perhaps something more. She was staying in my quarters, after all.

I flipped a hand to dismiss his concerns. "It is fine. The female needs all the help she can get when it comes to Zindar."

Sloane gasped in mock outrage, which pleased me.

"I'll have you know that Taron here told me I was close to winning when you left."

I fought the urge to laugh as Taron shifted from one foot to the other. "Did he?"

The Vandar moved to the door, giving Sloane a quick glance. "Good luck, human." He clicked his heels in another salute to me. "Raas."

Once the door had slid shut on him, I turned back to Sloane.

"I'm ready for a rematch."

I glanced at the game board and then at her. Even in her utilitarian flight suit that hid almost any trace of the curves I'd seen on full display when she'd been in my bed, the female made my heart pound. I would have preferred to rip her flight suit off her and drag her to my bed instead of playing Zindar, but I took the chair across from her.

"Since you have the advantage of a lesson in Zindar strategy, maybe you'd be willing to make a wager on our game?"

Her eyebrows popped up. "What kind of a wager?"

"If I win, you join me in the pools. But this time you do as I wish."

She bit her bottom lip. "And if I win?"

I doubted she would defeat me in only her second game, even with tips from another Vandar, but I tilted my head. "What do you wish?"

"A tour of the ship," she said, leaning back and grinning. "You show me around your warbird—all of it."

She wanted me to allow her to see all of a Vandar warbird? One of the reasons we didn't take prisoners was to prevent foreign eyes from glimpsing how our birds were laid out and how they worked. Now a human prisoner wished to get a personal tour from the Raas? I almost scoffed out loud.

Then thoughts of claiming her in the warm waters of the bathing pool flooded my mind. I would agree to just about anything to hasten that reality. "It seems we have another deal."

CHAPTER
TWENTY-FIVE

Ronnan

"You are sure you wish to move there?" I eyed the female's delicate fingers lingering on the game piece.

She shifted her gaze to me, her expression wavering for a moment before a grin spilt her face. She lifted her hand and sat back. "Nice try, Vandar."

I cocked one eyebrow. Vandar? The minx was getting confident, no doubt helped along by her simperingly excellent gamesmanship. I wouldn't admit it out loud, but she was a natural at Zindar. Maybe she was right about her flying skill helping her when it came to strategy, or maybe my fellow Kyrie Vandar's tips had been more valuable than I'd anticipated. Had I ever played against Taron? I wasn't sure but I'd have to be sure to challenge him to a match soon, if only to learn how he'd imparted so much knowledge of the game so quickly.

Sloane propped her elbows on the table and leaned on her folded hands. "Your move, Raas."

Hearing her call me by my title sent an electric thrill through me, but I tempered my desire and focused on the board. I wasn't sure how long we'd been playing, but the human had lasted longer than I'd imagined. What I'd assumed would be an easy win on my part had turned into a back-and-forth battle with all my attempts to defeat her deftly avoided.

To become Raas, I'd had to overcome many hurdles and challenges, both from Vandar elders and from my fellow raiders. I'd grown accustomed to winning, although Sloane's challenge was different from any other. Watching her try to beat me was thrilling. It was like she was resisting my ultimate domination, and I relished her struggle. I would still enjoy exerting myself over her more, though.

I saw my opening on the board and moved, watching with satisfaction as the board shifted, elevating my pieces closer to the top. Before I could lean back and savor the moment, Sloane's eyes widened, and she straightened in her seat.

I swung my gaze back to the board. What had she seen that I'd missed?

Then I saw it. The opening that would allow her to move within striking distance of the pinnacle position. *Tvek*. I'd been too distracted by thoughts of having my way with Sloane and now I might lose to her—and lose the prize of claiming her in the bathing pools.

I could almost hear my father's gruff voice warning me not to be distracted by things as unimportant as females. I pushed it aside. As much as I'd valued his military advice, I'd hated the way he'd talked about mates as if they were nothing. It had always felt like a betrayal of my mother and all the Selkee mates, and I'd despised him a little more every time he'd said it.

But you still listened, a dark voice hissed from the recesses of my brain. As much as I'd hated him for his mercenary view on females and mates, I'd avoided Selkee females and any entanglement that might distract me from my mission—the mission I'd been given by my father.

Until now. I looked up at Sloane as she gleefully moved her game piece. How had I allowed a female as unexpected and unassuming as this one to creep into my heart? She wasn't even a trained pleasurer skilled in the art of seduction. Nevertheless, she now consumed my thoughts and had rattled my focus enough that I was on the verge of losing a game of Zindar to her.

When her piece locked into place, the board moved once again. Instead of promoting her to the top spot, the panels overlapped so that our pieces were both eliminated. They fell to the table with a clatter.

"Fuck me!" Sloane smacked her hand on the table before catching the pieces rolling toward the edge. "I had you!"

I exhaled and allowed myself a grin. "Now we appear to have a stalemate. Neither of us can win."

She frowned. "That's possible?"

"Possible and not uncommon. Neither of us lose and neither of us win."

"So, a tie?" She bobbled her head. "I can live with that."

"I hope so, because that means we both win our wager and we both lose."

Her jaw fell open. "We don't rematch?"

As long as the game had taken, I had no patience for a rematch. Not when she might very well win and not have to pay up her end of the bargain.

"No rematch until all scores from our first wager have been paid." I stood and took her hand, pulling her from her chair.

She spluttered as I led her toward the bathing chamber. "What about my tour of the ship?"

"First things first," I said as we passed through the arched doorway and into the dim, black-stone room lit by the blue star chart embedded in the ceiling.

"Who made that rule?"

I stopped in front of the sunken pool and pivoted her to face me. "Did you forget that I am Raas, and I make all the rules within my horde?"

Her eyes were round as she shook her head. "I thought..."

"That you could win your freedom from me?" I shook my head as I slid the zipper down the front of her flight suit. "Not so easily. It will take more than a game to convince me to let you go."

She didn't break my gaze as I slid the fabric from her body, feathering my hands across her petal-soft skin to remove her undergarments. Then I unhooked my belt and battle kilt before kicking off my boots.

I took her hand again to lead her into the steaming water. "Time to fulfill your end of the bargain."

CHAPTER
TWENTY-SIX

Sloane

y pulse fluttered as he led me down the stairs into the water, but I kept my gaze locked onto his broad back. If I looked farther down, I would lose my nerve and try to run. It didn't matter that I'd already been with the alien. Seeing how big he was made my nerves jangle and my pussy twinge. Would I even be able to stand after I left his captivity?

A slightly hysterical laugh bubbled up in my throat as I imagined having to be carried from the Vandar warbird because I'd fucked their warlord too much. That was not how I wanted to return to my fellow resistance fighters.

And I did want to return to the Valox resistance, didn't I?

Part of me was enjoying the luxurious bath and sumptuous bed that being the Raas' prisoner afforded me. Even the food was better than what I'd become used to on the Valox base.

Come on Sloane, I chided myself. You aren't so weak that a few creature comforts would make you abandon your mission and friends. *My friends.* My mind went to Cassie and Thea. By now, they would definitely know something was wrong. If they weren't personally searching for me, they would have at least alerted the Valox leadership. All while I was spending my time playing a game and banging an alien warlord.

"This can't be so distasteful," Ronnan said, when we were standing in the water, and he'd turned to face me.

I realized that I'd been frowning as I'd thought of my disloyal actions. I shook my head, although that didn't rid me of the uneasy feeling. "I was just thinking that my friends are probably searching for me and worried I'm dead."

The Vandar made a humming sound that was half dismissive and half sympathetic. "You shouldn't think about them now."

Easier said than done, although the heat of the water was making it easy for my troubles to slip away. Ronnan took both of my hands and pulled me down so that I was submerged to my chin. Then he tugged me close to him, wrapping my legs around his waist as he backed up until he was sitting on a built-in stone seat on the wall I hadn't even noticed before.

I was facing the Vandar, our faces at the same level and the water lapping between our bodies. The hard bar of his cock jutted up behind my bare ass, and I was very aware of it as I straddled him.

"Once you settle your score with the other Vandar, you won't need me for leverage anymore, right?"

The Raas' brows pressed together, but he grunted what I took as a yes. "But until then, you are mine."

My heart raced as his hands slid to grip my hips. Why did the stakes seem higher now than they had when I'd woken with him in bed with me? I'd been fully aware of what I'd been doing then, but somehow this seemed more like playing with fire. Maybe because there was a difference between a one-off fling and something I couldn't get enough of, even though I knew it was dangerous.

"What about our deal?" I croaked.

"This was the deal if you lost. Since neither of us won, this is how you're settling your wager."

"Not that deal." I met his gaze as I placed my hands on his shoulders. "The one about neither of us falling for the other."

Another rough grunt as he pulled me forward so that my breasts brushed his chest. "I am fucking you, not falling for you."

I swallowed hard. "Good, because you know I'm not staying."

Ronnan threaded one hand in my hair, jerking my head back so he could nip at the exposed skin on my throat. With the other hand, he lifted my body and notched me over the thick head of his cock. "Too much talking."

I didn't have time to respond before he was driving me down on him. I gasped as he impaled my body on his rigid length, my fingers biting into his flesh as he bit my neck. Pleasure and pain shot through me, mingling in a strange dance that sent desire barreling through me.

I tried to tear myself from his grasp, but the Vandar held me to him. He worked his mouth up until he'd captured mine, opening my lips to him. Our tongues tangled, mine fighting for dominance even as he proved himself to be stronger than me and able to use my body for his pleasure.

But it wasn't only his pleasure. I moaned as unwanted pulses of euphoria surged through me, pleasure pounding a relentless drumbeat as Ronnan moved me up and down his thick cock. I was helpless to the sensations he provoked, as much as I wished to fight them and fight him. I should be resisting him, but I was at the mercy of his body's demands and my own body's hunger for him.

My resistance to him—what it was—faded the longer I was in the water, until I could barely remember why I hadn't wanted this. He filled me like no one ever had, and his dominant desires filled an emptiness I hadn't known existed.

My fingers scored his shoulders as I rocked into him, and his kisses became primal and all-consuming. When he ripped his lips from mine, he pinned me with a velvet stare. His rhythm had turned savage, as both of his hands clutched my hips as if they were a lifeline.

"Why do you have to be so perfect?" He growled, as the water splashed violently around us and our bodies slapped together under the surface.

I was teetering too close to the edge to speak, my breaths desperate as a torrent of sensations stormed through me.

"You will always be mine," the Vandar husked, as he arched his back and thrust up. "Won't you, Sloane?"

Heat rolled over me as I nodded.

"Say it," he commanded. "Say you belong to me."

"I belong to you, Raas," I cried as my body spasmed around his cock, and he exploded inside me.

They were only words, but at that moment, they were the most honest thing I'd ever said.

TWENTY-SEVEN

Ronnan

"I can't walk around in this." Sloane looked down at the fabric kilt I'd belted around her waist. A loose tunic was tucked into the kilt and the sleeves rolled up, so the material didn't sag off her small frame. Her own black boots were on her feet, although Vandar battle boots would have looked better.

"Why not?" I cut my eyes to the bathing chamber behind us where her flight suit lay on the floor in a puddle. Her only clothing had fallen victim to our vigorous splashing.

"I look like a...a..."

"A Vandar," I finished for her, my voice humming with a strange pride that the human did look a bit like a Vandar warrior.

Her brows peaked and then she frowned. "I look like I'm playing dress-up."

Now I cocked my head at her. "Dress-up?"

She shook her head. "Something little girls play with clothes that are too big for them."

"You are hardly a little girl." She might be smaller than any Vandar, but she'd proven she was no little girl by how well she'd taken me. The thought stirred heat in my core and made me almost forget my promise. "But you could always choose to wear nothing for your tour of the warbird. I would not mind."

She shot me a dark look. "No, thank you. I guess I'll be a mini-Vandar for now."

I fought the urge to drag her to my bed, flip her kilt up, and take her from behind. The sight of the feminine human in the traditional Vandar battle garb was more arousing than I'd imagined it could be, and it didn't help that so much of her long legs were bare. Memories of them hooked over my shoulders made my cock twitch to life, even though I should have been spent after fucking in the bathing pools.

"Ready to play tour guide?" Sloane asked, snapping me back to reality.

I tightened my own belt and hooked my battle axe on my waist as I strode to the door with her at my side. "Remember what I told you."

She released a breath, not bothering to hide her impatience. "No touching anything. No asking questions of your raiders. No distracting them from their duties."

I gave a curt nod to the warriors guarding the door as we passed through it. They appeared slightly startled, either at Sloane's attire, or the fact that she was leaving with me, but they clicked their heels in salute and said nothing. A Vandar raider would never question their Raas, no matter how crazy they believed his actions to be—and there could be a strong argument that what I was doing was mad.

Not only was the female the first non-Vandar to come aboard our warbird, she was the only creature to be allowed to see how our ship was constructed and how it worked. The design of our vessels—and our invisibility shielding technology—were closely guarded secrets. To share that with anyone who was not one of us was not done. So, why was I doing it?

I thought back to our wager over the Zindar board. First, I hadn't believed for a moment that she would win the bet. Then I'd been so preoccupied by getting what I wanted from the deal—her submitting to my will in the bathing pools—that I hadn't let myself think about the promise I'd made.

She's no threat, I told myself as I led her deeper into the warbird, spiraling down open staircases and jumping from one platform to the other as she held my hand to keep from plummeting into the cavernous core of the vessel. Booming voices and clanging metal echoed around us as we delved into the bowels of the warbird, the temperature rising as we drew closer to the engines.

Sloane was a member of the resistance fighters who'd fought *with* the Vandar, I reassured myself. She had no reason to be a threat to us, even if we were not exactly on friendly terms with the Vandar of this sector.

Besides, she was still my captive. It didn't matter what she learned of our ship. She would not be telling anyone. Not when she was still under my control. My pulse tripped as I thought of more delicious ways I'd like to exert my control over her.

Then I thought of my promises to her friends and my ardor cooled. I'd vowed to release her if they brought me a Vandar horde, but would I? Could I turn her over so easily after everything? The idea of her leaving my quarters and my bed and never returning made a knot harden in my gut.

A blast of steam snapped me from my mental wanderings.

Sloane held a hand up to her nose as we entered the engineering bay. "What is this place?"

"You wanted to see everything." I waved at the chrome machines that whirred and hummed around a central clear cylinder that swirled with vividly colored light. "This is how our horde flies so swiftly and slips through space like wraiths."

She blinked rapidly, clearly impressed. "How does it work?"

I found myself filled with an unusual burst of pride for my vessel. I enjoyed showing her what I commanded, and I was proud of my raiders' achievements. I was also suddenly aware of the engineering crew emerging from behind their consoles and staring at us. I took Sloane by the elbow and pulled her outside again. "You do not need to know that any more than you need to know how your own ships are built."

"I don't know. If I'd paid more attention to the mechanics of my ship, I might not have been stranded in space for you to find me."

I ignored this, grateful that she hadn't learned more about mechanics. I led her to a lift that was little more than a platform being raised by a creaky pulley system, stepping on and pulling her with me. There was barely enough room for me, so I had to wrap one arm and my tail around her to keep her steady as I held the center beam while we were lifted into the air.

She buried her face in my chest as the floor dropped away. "This is the most terrifying elevator I've ever seen."

"It is faster." I didn't tell her that I doubted her ability to keep up as we wound our way up the entire span of the ship considering her shorter legs.

When we'd almost drawn even with a platform, I leapt from the lift, bringing her with me as the pulley continued to move ever higher.

"Where are we now?" Sloane gave herself a brief shake as I released my tight grip on her and unwound my tail from her legs.

I proceeded down a suspended walkway that swayed beneath our feet and then through a wide, open archway. Another blast of steam hit me, but this time it carried savory scents with it.

"The kitchens," Sloane said before I could tell her.

The space was probably the most bustling one on the ship with cooks moving between open flames and stirring enormous pots. Trays of bread sat cooling on open racks, filling the air with the yeasty aroma and making my stomach rumble.

When we entered, the frenetic movement seemed to freeze. Every cook stared at us, their startled gazes shifting from me to Sloane. I plucked a couple of rolls from a rack, nodded at the cooks, and backed us from the room.

Sloane took the warm bread I proffered. "I'm getting the sense that you don't have many visitors or give many tours."

I grunted as I tore off a bite of bread with my teeth, the pillowy texture almost sensual as I swallowed. "You are the first."

We chewed in silence as I led her back down the walkway. "The lift or a climb?" I asked, gesturing first to the pulley system moving toward the top of the warbird and then to a series of winding metal staircases.

She popped the last bit of bread in her mouth. "Definitely the stairs."

"Hold the railings," I told her as I started up in front of her. Some of the stairs twisted over the open chasm in the middle of the ship, and there was nothing to catch a fall but more steel bars below.

I tempered my pace, making sure she was behind me with each careful step instead of taking them several steps at a time or with a single leap as I usually did. At the top, I paused and held out my hand. She took it and allowed me to lead her through arched doors that glided open and onto the command deck.

I'd expected to show her the impressive view of space that my perch afforded, but instead of a vast array of twinkling stars, the view screen was taken up by the faces of the Valox females we'd encountered before.

"Sloane?" One of the females cried, spotting her before she'd had a chance to react to the sight of them. "You *are* alive!"

Sloane dropped my hand and rushed forward, ignoring the Vandar raiders at their posts, and my *majak* and battle chief gaping at both of us. "Cassie? Thea? How is this possible?"

The human female with blue hair smiled widely, her eyes glistening. "We're here to take you back. We did what Raas Ronnan asked us to do to secure your release."

Sloane stiffened. I couldn't see her face, but I could feel her confusion and then her anger as she whirled on me.

TWENTY-EIGHT

Sloane

T spun to face Ronnan, my fingers tingling with fury as I curled them into fists. "You made contact with my friends and didn't tell me?"

Every raider on the bridge pivoted to watch what was unfolding, and I could even feel Cassie's and Thea's gazes on us from the screen. Aside from the static and beeping of the computers and monitors, the room went quiet.

The Raas crossed his arms over his broad chest and his expression hardened. Whatever tenderness I'd glimpsed from him before was gone, replaced by the fierce warlord I'd first encountered. "You are a captive of the Vandar. You make no demands here."

I should have stopped while I was ahead, but I was too irate to listen to my instincts. "You still consider me a prisoner? After everything?"

The raider I knew as his first officer stepped closer to Ronnan, tapping his heels together. "Should we continue this discussion in your strategy room, Raas?"

Ronnan's pupils flared as he stared me down. He did not want to give even a micron, but he finally glanced at the warrior and grunted. Without a word, he turned on his heel so fast his kilt smacked his thighs and headed toward a smaller door still within the command deck. "Bring her."

I didn't need to be escorted, so when the Vandar who'd first taken me to his torture chamber advanced on me, I sidestepped his grasp. "I can walk by myself, thank you very much."

The two Vandar exchanged glances as they followed their Raas and me. The door slid open silently and we all processed inside, with me shooting the other guys dirty looks behind Ronnan's back. It might not be their fault, but I was sure they'd known about the deal he'd made with Cassie and Thea, so for me, they were all complicit.

Once the door shut behind us, the Raas swiveled around to face me, his face still stony.

"You lied to me," I said before he could open his mouth.

"I did not lie."

Okay, technically he hadn't lied to me, since I'd never thought to ask him if he'd made contact with my best friends and coerced them to bring a Vandar horde to him in exchange for my freedom. How would that have ever occurred to me?

I huffed out a breath. "You purposefully omitted information you knew I'd want to know."

He tilted his head slowly at me. "You seem to think you aren't a captive of the Kyrie Vandar anymore. I told you exactly why I'd taken you prisoner and what I wanted from you—leverage so we could entice the Vandar into negotiations."

I opened my mouth then closed it again. He was right. He'd been upfront about wanting to use me—first to get information on the location of the Vandar, which I didn't have, and then as a pawn to lure the Vandar to them. Why had I forgotten that?

Because you thought things had changed, a small voice whispered in the back of my brain. You thought he wouldn't use you because you'd become something more to him.

Which I clearly hadn't.

"I'm still nothing but a pawn to you?"

Ronnan's gaze softened for a heartbeat then his expression shuttered again. The Raas I thought I'd known was back to being the hard, cold warlord who'd first ordered me to his bed.

"Have you been mistreated?" He clasped his hands behind his back and walked toward the glass wall. "I think we've established that you haven't been lied to."

I pressed my lips together, refusing to answer. If he could be cold and heartless, so could I, especially since my throat was tight, and I was afraid if I tried to speak, I might cry.

When he reached the glass, he craned his neck to glance at me. I turned my head and refused to meet his gaze. I would not let him see the tears that were threatening to spill from my eyes, even as they stung the backs of my lids.

"You should be glad you were not turned over to my care," the other raider growled. "You would not have been so comfortable in my *oblek*. Or so fully clothed."

The first officer made a disapproving noise in the back of his throat. "The fact remains that the Valox have returned, and they claim to have told the Vandar—and that the Vandar have agreed to a rendezvous."

"They fulfilled their end of the deal then?" Ronnan asked, his voice not as victorious as it should have been.

"We haven't seen the Vandar yet," the other officer said, crossing his arms and shifting his weight from one leg to the other. "They could be lying."

I hoped they were, but I doubted that Cassie and Thea would lie if my life was at stake. Somehow, they must have tracked down a Vandar contact and convinced them to come. My debt to my friends was growing by the moment.

"I doubt the females would put their friend's life at risk," Ronnan said, mirroring my own thoughts, which was seriously annoying. "But I do not know them well." He slid his gaze to me. "Would your fellow rebels be so careless with your safety?"

I glared at him, wishing I could shoot actual daggers with my eyes, but I refused to answer, jerking my head from him and gazing at the wall. I'd been the one who'd been careless, but I didn't intend to make that mistake again.

The only silver lining was the growing possibility that I would be leaving the Vandar ship. As soon as the Vandar were sure they'd gotten what they wanted, I would be free. Apparently, that had been the deal and the thought of being with my best friends again dampened my fury.

"Raas," his first officer's voice was both filled with awe and shock as he gazed past Ronnan and out the window. "They did not lie."

An entire horde of silver Vandar ships were materializing from the darkness, the sides of the enormous vessels spread wide as if they were wings on terrifying birds of prey.

CHAPTER
TWENTY-NINE

Ronnan

M y heart pounded even as my fingers tingled in anticipation. They'd come. After spending my entire life planning and preparing for this moment, it had finally arrived. We were finally facing off with the Vandar.

"Holy shit," Sloane whispered, as her gaze was drawn to the view of the menacing warbirds hovering in space. She walked closer to the narrow wall of glass in my strategy room, placing her fingers on the surface. "I've never seen a horde of Vandar ships before."

My chest swelled in a strange sort of pride. The horde looked just as ours did, after all, and the Vandar warbirds were a thing of terrifying beauty. Then I remembered why the other Vandar were here and why the human should not be.

I slid my gaze to her back as she stared at Vandar fleet in open-mouthed awe. My stomach clenched at what I was about to do, but it had to be done. An entire generation of Kyrie Vandar had given up everything and everyone they knew to traverse the galaxy and fulfill our destiny. As Raas, I could not allow a single female to derail this.

It had been a mistake to open myself to Sloane, especially since I knew there could be no future for us. Not if I was to fulfill my father's wish of restoring the Vandar bloodline. And after coming this far and paying such a high price, there could be no other choice. Falling for the human had never been an option, and allowing myself to even dabble with the thought of keeping her had been an indulgence that now filled me with shame.

My face flamed as I remembered thinking I could continue our dalliances in the pool and our challenges across the Zindar board. Had I really believed that I could keep a human as a plaything—or worse, take her as a mate? Some of the other Vandar might have succumbed to the shockingly appealing creatures, but I could not allow myself such a weakness. Not if I was going to be the Raas who restored the Kyrie Vandar to their rightful place.

I had already allowed myself to be weakened by my tender feelings toward the female. It had done nothing but confuse my fellow raiders and muddle my own mind. She had been my captive and she'd served her purpose. Anything more had been a foolish dream, and it was time to kill it once and for all.

I jerked my gaze from Sloane, meeting the questioning eyes of my *majak* and battle chief as they stood in respectful but anxious silence. "It seems the rebels did not lie. We will return the captive to them—once our negotiations have concluded." I flicked a hand and pivoted on my heel to return to the command deck. "Take her to my quarters to await her transport."

Kaiven gave me an appreciative nod, releasing a heavy breath. "It is done, Raas."

"Wait, what?" Sloane's voice stopped me before I reached the door. "That's it? You got what you needed and now you're tossing me out like the trash."

I turned slowly to face her, my gut in a hard ball as I steeled my expression. If I'd expected her to be grateful that she was going back to her Valox resistance, as promised, I was sorely mistaken. She appeared just as livid as she'd been when she thought she might not be able to leave, which only reinforced my belief that human females made no sense. "You wished to be returned to your friends. You have desired nothing but to be free since you were brought on board this warbird. I am not tossing you out. I am merely granting your request."

Her eyes flashed. "Just like that?"

I met her gaze, the hard ball in my stomach only churning more as I recognized the pain in her eyes. Pain that would soon be forgotten by both of us, I reminded myself. I drew in a breath. "You will remain in my quarters until we have completed our deal with the Vandar, and I will arrange for food to be brought to you before your departure."

"Unbelievable," she muttered, shaking her head. Then she narrowed her eyes at me. "If you're so ready to return me, why not do it now? Let's not drag this out, Raas. It's not like your quarters hold any special memories for me. I'm happy to head to the hangar bay and wait there."

Her eagerness to be free of me and her comment about my quarters sparked my ire, and I stepped closer to her and lowered my voice. "You could wait in my battle chief's *oblek*."

She lunged for me with her hand raised, but Ayden caught her arm before it made contact with me.

"I do not suggest that course of action." His voice was steady but held a note of warning.

Sloane seemed to deflate as my *majak* slowly released his grip on her. "Whatever." She cut her gaze to Kaiven. "Let's go."

My battle chief stepped forward to take hold of her, but she marched past him and me without a glance at either of us, her shoulders squared, and her head held high. I fought the urge to reach for her, but what was the point? It was better for her to despise me anyway. Hate would prevent any chance of heartbreak.

Kaiven caught up to her with a couple of long strides, and he led her from my strategy room and across the command deck. My heart sank as I watched her go, but I swallowed the bitter taste of my own heartbreak and shook it off with a visible shudder.

Ayden raised his eyebrows at me, but when he opened his mouth to speak, I waved any question away. "It is done. Now we deal with the Vandar."

My *majak* gave a single, curt nod. He knew me well enough to know when a matter was closed, and the matter of the female captive was done for good.

We returned to the command deck and stood shoulder to shoulder on the raised platform as all the raiders at their posts looked to me for guidance.

"We have traveled long and far for this day," I said, my voice rising. "It is time for the Kyrie Vandar to take what is rightfully ours."

Murmurs of agreement rippled through the deck as legs were set wide and shoulders were squared.

"All glory to Lokken, god of old," I intoned the ancient battle cry like a mantra.

The raiders surrounding me raised their battle axes. "Glory to Lokken!"

The echo of the chant reverberated through my bones, giving me strength as I flicked a gaze at my communications chief. "Open a channel to the lead horde ship."

"Yes, Raas." His fingers tapped rapidly on the console, and his head snapped up almost as fast. "They have responded."

I took a steadying breath. "On screen."

Our view of the array of horde ships disappeared and was replaced by the sight of a Vandar raider with long, jet-black hair and heavy, black-leather shoulder armor that looked like scales. His hands were braced on his hips, and his face was set in a scowl I knew all too well.

After carefully stoking my fury for so long, I had prepared myself to face off against a Vandar raider who looked so much like my own father and all the original Vandar exiles I'd grown up around. From the sharp intakes of breath around me, I knew my fellow raiders were experiencing the same uncomfortable sensation of familiarity.

Of course, we'd known we were returning to our kin, but after living among the Selkee and other aliens for our entire lives, seeing our fathers reflected in the Vandar we were challenging was like cold water on my fiery rage.

Still, I curled my hands into fists as I met the hard gaze of the Vandar. "To whom am I speaking?"

He was clearly a Raas, and one of his dark brows arched in malevolent amusement. "I am Raas Kaalek of the Vandar. The more important question is, who are you, and why have you dared summon a Vandar horde?"

I rested one hand on the hilt of my axe, the cold steel grounding me and reminding me of my purpose. I recited the words that had been drilled into me since I'd been at my father's knee. "I am Raas Ronnan of the Kyrie Vandar. We have returned to take what was stolen from us, and to lay claim to our rightful place with the Vandar."

The raider with leather and metal straps crisscrossing his chest blinked rapidly. "Kyrie Vandar? You are the Lost Vandar?" He squinted and stepped closer, as if trying to get a better look at us. "Then the stories were true."

CHAPTER
THIRTY

Sloane

I didn't wait until the door to the Raas' quarters slid shut on Kaiven's smug face before I unleashed a string of curses on both him and the door. "Cocky asshole can kiss my..." I thrust one arm up at him in a rude gesture, but he was already gone.

I spun around and began to stomp furiously across the glossy floors. I was livid at the arrogant battle chief who'd escorted me through the ship because he was clearly pleased that Ronnan had sent me away, but I was angrier at Ronnan, himself. My eyes stung with hot tears, but I tipped my head back and blinked at the ceiling, refusing to let them fall.

"I'm not crying over that asshole."

But my eyes were swimming as I pressed the heels of my hands to my eyes and fought the urge to sob. How had I been so stupid? Had I actually believed that banging the alien warlord who was holding me as his prisoner would turn out any other way?

Memories of his furtive words whispered hot in my ear reminded me of why I'd allowed myself to be tricked by him. He'd said all the right things and pretended to be exactly what I'd wanted him to be. It didn't matter that he'd said I belonged to him. That had all been part of the game. It hadn't been real.

My heart twisted as the depth of my stupidity hit me. I'd allowed myself to fall for the alien after I'd promised myself I wouldn't. I knew what it was like to lose someone, and I'd still opened my heart to him.

"Idiot," I muttered, swiping away the hot tears that had slipped from beneath my hands. I'd known better than to trust him. He was a violent Vandar warlord, after all. Aside from the few who'd bucked their traditions and taken human mates, they weren't exactly known for being the type of aliens who fell in love.

I cringed at the word as soon as I thought it. I didn't love him —did I?

I shook my head vigorously, as if trying to rid myself of any trace of feelings I'd had for Ronnan. I hadn't known him long enough to love him, had I? My love for Leo had grown slowly over a long period of time, and it had been a friendship that had eventually morphed into something else. What I'd had with the Raas was completely different.

My face burned as memories of being entangled with the huge Vandar flooded my mind, his cock buried in me so deep I'd thought we'd become one. I might not have known him long, but there was no use denying that our time had been passionate and intense. Even now, I could almost feel his hands scorching my skin as he gripped my hips and drove into me.

I groaned, half of me wanting to purge my mind from all thoughts of him and half wanting him to burst into the room and bury himself in me.

"That isn't going to happen," I reminded myself, shaking out my arms. "You're not going to see him again. He's done with you."

The pain of that realization made me almost double over, but I welcomed it. Better to get it out of my system now, than return to the resistance and my friends, broken up over the warlord who'd been my captor. That would not go over well with my fellow rebels.

I should be glad I was going home. It was what I'd wanted, as the Raas had so coldly reminded me. Part of me had thought that he wouldn't let me go no matter what happened, or how much my presence as a pawn got them what they wanted. And a tiny part of me had wanted him to keep me.

I huffed out an impatient breath. "Enough of this. You're being ridiculous. Be glad you'll see Cassie and Thea soon and be far away from all the Vandar drama."

Once I was free, I could return to my search for the Zagrath, although I had a feeling I would no longer be allowed to fly recon missions solo. That was okay, too. Maybe Cassie and Thea would be so happy to see me I could guilt them into coming with me.

This thought made me smile. I could almost picture Thea rolling her eyes, and Cassie enthusiastically agreeing and making Thea feign enthusiasm. I really had missed my friends and would be happy to see them again. I started to hum some Bon Jovi as I walked to the floor-to-ceiling glass that made up the far wall.

"You give love a bad name," I sang softly, as I watched the Vandar horde and wondered what was happening on the bridge. Would Ronnan finally get what he wanted?

"Not your concern anymore, Sloane." I hummed more of the old song as the music drained the anger from me and steadied my heartbeat.

I glanced at my outfit. Since I was leaving the Vandar, there was no point in dressing like one. I scanned the space and located my flight suit draped across the bed. I grinned at the familiar outfit, striding quickly to it.

It was dry, and even looked like it had been cleaned in the time we'd been gone. I eagerly removed the nubby-fabric kilt and tunic, and I stepped into the dark jumpsuit. It might be well-worn, but it represented a lot of successful missions.

I ran my hands down the front of it. "Let's go home."

It was time to return to my life and forget about the Vandar and try to forget Raas Ronnan. Time to be a Valox pilot again. I thought about the promises the Raas had elicited from me, the ones I'd meant when I'd said them, and the promises he'd made to me. I swallowed the sour taste of betrayal and lies.

"No more deals," I whispered to myself. "And all bets are off."

THIRTY-ONE

Ronnan

Silence hung in the air of the command deck as Raas Kaalek's words sank in. "Stories? You know of the Kyrie Vandar?"

The dark-haired Vandar folded his arms over his chest and grunted, the gesture so familiar it almost made me flinch. "Maybe I should say that we heard whispers, not stories." His frown deepened. "I did not spend much time with my own father, but on more than one occasion I heard him and others mention the Vandar who'd left—the lost Vandar."

"Left?" The hairs on my arms prickled. "You were told that we left?"

Kaalek's brow furrowed more deeply. "Are you saying the Vandar elders—and my father, Raas Bardon—lied?"

Despite the warning edge in his voice, I crossed my own arms and mirrored his stance. "I am. The Kyrie Vandar were only lost because we were cast out."

Even across the distance and the transmission, I could hear the dark murmurings on the Raas' command deck. Accusing a Raas of the Vandar—and his father—of lying was a serious breach in protocol. The accusatory slap had landed, and I braced myself for the violent rebuttal.

A muscle ticked in Raas Kaalek's jaw as he held my gaze, then he shocked me more than declaring war and firing all his missiles at us would have. He blew out a long breath and shook his head. "I am not surprised."

"What?" I spluttered before tempering my reaction.

Raas Kaalek let out a low, rumbling laugh. "There was a time not too long ago when I would have destroyed your entire horde for daring to speak ill of another Raas, but I am a different Vandar, now."

I wondered if this had to do with him taking a human mate. Was his Raisa the one with the fiery temper or the one who'd been taken as a war prize?

"My father was a brutal Raas," Kaalek continued, "and not only to our enemies. It does not shock me to learn that he was involved in cruelly exiling your ancestors."

This was not going as I'd expected it to. I'd prepared myself for violence and threats, not understanding. My throat was thick with emotion as the burden of our legacy slowly released its grip on me.

"Our fathers disagreed with the decisions of some of the Raases. They rose in challenge, and when they were defeated, they were exiled from the hordes and from Vandar space."

Kaalek pressed his lips together. "The elders never spoke of exile. Where did you go?"

I knew the story as well as if I'd lived it, but the words felt thick in my mouth. "Our fathers were chased to the farthest sector where they found a planet that welcomed them. They took Selkee mates and started families, but all the while building a Vandar horde so they could one day return and exact vengeance."

Kaalek's pupils flared. "Is that why you have come? Vengeance for the sins of our long-dead fathers?"

Looking at the Vandar through the screen made my heart ache for belonging. I did not want to fight this Raas. He had committed no sin.

"We have returned to take our rightful place among you. We are Vandar, and we do not wish to be lost anymore."

I avoided glancing at my *majak* or anyone else on the command deck. If they believed we should battle our Vandar brothers instead of joining with them, I did not want to know it. I was Raas, and my word was law.

"My own brothers and I were estranged for many moons, because of our father's brutality and desire for dominance over all things," Raas Kaalek said, his voice gravelly. "The entire Vandar empire was fragmented because of the old Raases and their hunger for control, but it did not make us strong. Only when we joined together did we become mighty enough to defeat the Zagrath."

I inclined my head at him, feeling a kinship for this Vandar who had also come from a fractured family and a domineering father. "We have heard much of your victory."

"It was done with all the hordes, rebels from many planets, resistance fighters, and bounty hunters. We owe all our allies a great debt." His expression darkened. "Which is why I must request that you release the human prisoner and return her to the Valox."

Even though my plan had always been to release Sloane once I'd gotten what I wanted, I hesitated in responding. I might have sent her away with promises that she would be on the next transport off the warbird, but once I agreed to her release, it was over.

"Raas." My *majak* spoke for the first time since we'd opened the channel with the Vandar, but his voice was so hushed I suspected only I could hear him. "You should make the deal. This is what we came for."

Ayden was right. This was why we'd flown across the galaxy. If I wished to be revered as Raas, I needed to put the horde first. Even above my own desires.

"Agreed," I said loudly, and I sensed my *majak* relax beside me.

"I assume the prisoner has been unharmed." Raas Kaalek gave me a knowing look that made my skin heat.

"She has been well attended to," I said, returning his gaze.

Kaalek grunted, the corners of his mouth quirking. "They are a surprisingly challenging species, considering their stature and lack of natural defenses. My horde kept a female human as a prisoner once. We barely survived."

"Is this the human you took as Raisa?" I asked.

His eyes widened slightly. "It's clear you know much more about us than we know about you."

I shrugged. "It was necessary."

Kaalek nodded, shifting his weight from one leg to another, his battle kilt swaying. "It seems we have much to learn about you, our returned Vandar brothers. Transfer the human to my ship, and then you and your command staff will be guests at a welcoming banquet."

I flicked a glance at Kaiven as he strode onto the command deck. "Battle chief, our female prisoner will be leaving us now. I need her to be delivered to the lead Vandar warbird."

He barely broke stride as he pivoted back toward the arched doorway. "It is done, Raas—gladly."

Part of me wished to see Sloane one more time before she was gone forever, but I knew it would only prolong the torture. Besides, she was already furious at me. It was easier for both of us if she left believing me to be cruel and heartless. There was no point in her knowing that my chest ached as I watched my battle chief stalk off, knowing that he would do exactly as I'd ordered.

I twisted to face Raas Kaalek. "It is done."

He snapped his heels sharply in salute to me. How long had the Kyrie Vandar waited to be acknowledged like this, to be welcomed back into the fold? I returned the salute by rapping the heels of my boots together. I swiveled my gaze across my command deck, giving my raiders a curt nod. Then they all saluted Raas Kaalek in unison.

The unity of the Vandar was worth it, I assured myself. My sacrifice had been worth it. I attempted to focus on Kaalek's words as he told me of the recent battle to defeat the Zagrath and their current status as protectors of the sector, but my thoughts unwillingly wandered to Sloane.

Now that our mission had changed, did I care so much about my father's plan for me? Would I let his words hold power over me? I had to return Sloane as part of the deal, but maybe I could find her again. My stomach sank as I thought of her anger at me. Would it be possible to win her back? Was it too much to hope that I could regain my place in the Vandar world and keep the female?

I glanced up at the screen, aware that Kaalek had asked me a question. Before I could ask him to repeat himself, an explosion threw me violently to the floor.

CHAPTER
THIRTY-TWO

Sloane

I tapped my foot impatiently as I waited by the door. Hadn't it been long enough? What kind of negotiating took this long?

I peered out the glass again. The horde ships hadn't moved or fired. That was good sign, I guessed. My pulse fluttered as I wondered if the Raas had changed his mind about releasing me. Maybe he was in the middle of a massive standoff with the other Vandar because he was refusing to let me go. I imagined his eyes flashing as he announced in his sexy, commanding voice that he would never let me go and they'd have to kill him and his entire horde to get to me.

"Vaes!"

I jerked toward the door, startled to see a Vandar raider standing in the open arch and looking fierce. But it wasn't Ronnan. It was his battle chief. The one who'd wanted to keep me in his torture chamber. "What?"

"*Vaes,*" he barked again, scowling at me. "Come with me. You're leaving."

"I'm...?" My question drifted off as he glared and waved me from the Raas' quarters.

"Leaving." The Vandar finished my question for me. "Your release has been secured by the Vandar. Follow me to the hangar bay."

So much for a dramatic standoff. I was being summarily escorted to the hangar bay by the Vandar who disliked me the most. At least he hadn't come to drag me off to the *oblek*. Small favors, I thought, as I fell in step behind him.

Unlike Ronnan, his battle chief didn't offer his arm as we wound our way down into the depths of the ship, so I gripped any handrail I could find and watched my step. The iron railings were cold but comforting as I followed the Vandar across suspended walkways that trembled beneath our feet and down winding stairways that seemed to go on forever.

I was too busy trying to keep from plummeting to my death to think much about Raas Ronnan, which was good because every thought of him sent both anger and desire pulsing through me. Once we were striding down a level corridor again, I decided that I was glad it hadn't been Ronnan who'd come to take me back. This way, it was easy to leave. If I survived the battle chief leading me to the hangar bay, I'd be so grateful to be boarding a vessel to leave, I wouldn't think twice about the Raas. If I'd had to watch him as I walked onto a transport, I might have lost my nerve.

We finally entered the hangar bay, and the scent of scorched fuel and engine grease made my nose twitch. Now these were scents I knew and loved. My fingers twitched at the thought of flying again.

I quickly scanned the oil-stained floor. "I'm guessing the Raas won't be coming to see me off."

I'd meant it as a joke, but the battle chief scoffed loudly. "The Raas does not see his pleasurers again once he's done with them."

"I'm not a pleasurer," I snapped. "Not that there's anything wrong with sex work, but I don't do it. I'm a pilot."

He eyed me coolly. "You are like all the others he's brought on the warbird for his amusement. Just because you are also a pilot makes you no different."

His words were like a punch to the gut. I knew I'd been an idiot to believe Ronnan, but this reminded me once again that everything he'd said to me was total crap. I might have been duped by the warlord, but I wasn't going to take shit from *this* Vandar too.

"Yeah, well you're just like every overconfident asshole who thinks they're better and smarter than everyone else just because they have a dick." As soon as the words left my mouth, I wondered if I'd just ruined any chance I had of leaving the ship in one piece.

The Vandar blinked at me a few times and then grunted. "Maybe you aren't like the others."

Before I could ask if that was a compliment, the ship shook so violently we were both thrown to the floor, my hands hitting the cold surface so hard they stung.

"We are under attack." The alien growled as he pushed himself to his feet and pilots and mechanics ran toward ships while alarms wailed. "The Vandar have betrayed us."

I staggered to stand, bracing my hand against the nearest silver-hulled ship as I squinted to look out the wide mouth at the far end that opened onto space and hummed with an energy field that kept us all from being sucked out. I knew the ships that now appeared against the black curtain of space, and they weren't Vandar.

"You aren't under attack by the Vandar," I yelled at Ronnan's battle chief, as I pointed toward the hulking gray ships. "The Zagrath are back."

THIRTY-THREE

Ronnan

My ears rang and my palms burned from smacking hard on the floor to catch my fall. Sirens screamed overhead as blue lights flashed. For a moment, I stared down at the glowing blue of my hands and tried to process what had happened. Then I shook my head and pushed myself off the floor, swallowing the metallic taste of blood.

"Report!" I bellowed, as other raiders staggered to their feet around me.

I reached down and extended a hand to my *majak,* hoisting him up so he could stand beside me. The view screen no longer displayed Raas Kaalek. Only gray static buzzed across the surface, as all the systems on the command deck spluttered and screeched.

"A direct hit, Raas," one of Kaiven's battle raiders said in his absence. "Communications suffered the most damage. I've raised shields, which are still at partial capacity and raised invisibility shielding. We are currently moving in the amoeba formation to avoid further attacks."

The amoeba pattern wouldn't work long if our attacker was also Vandar, since they had created the evasive maneuver.

"What of our Vandar brothers?" I asked, bitterness dripping from my words.

"They have also initiated invisibility shielding, Raas."

Another hit shook our ship, and Ayden clutched my arm to keep me upright as the command deck trembled.

"Indirect hit. Minimal damage to the hull, Raas."

"What of our weapons?" I asked, touching my head and detecting something sticky at my temple. I pulled back my hand, crimson blood dampening my fingertips, and wiped them roughly on my kilt.

"Operational." The raider narrowed his eyes, as his fingers hovered above the console.

Rage and betrayal flamed hot within me. Raas Kaalek had lied to my face about reunification and contrition. He only pretended to regret the dark history between our fathers when all the while he'd been planning to attack us. Bile rose in the back of my throat, overpowering the tang of blood, as regret consumed me. How had I been taken in so easily?

I scraped a hand through my blood-matted hair. It made no sense. He hadn't even waited until Sloane was a returned before breaking his promises. Wouldn't his Valox allies be angry that he'd put their pilot in danger? Maybe these Vandar had no honor, after all.

More hits exploded around us, but our evasive pattern was proving to be effective, which was curious since our opponents were Vandar who knew the pattern like it was etched on their skin.

"Return fire, Raas?"

"Can sensors tell the type of weapon fired?" Ayden asked, before I could shout my order to return fire on the Vandar horde, invisible or not.

Tvek. I swung my head to him, startled he would speak for me. But he'd always been the one to use caution, when I preferred to barrel headlong into danger. It had been that way since we were boys, and his steady temperament was the reason I was alive today.

Another raider frowned at his console. "The torpedo signature was not Vandar." He tapped furiously at the glossy surface that now boasted a crack along one side. "Unless our sensors are malfunctioning."

I growled in frustration, curling my fingers around the cold steel hilt of my battle axe. "Are they?"

The Vandar raised his head and shook it, his silvery-blond hair swinging. "No. The attack did not come from the Vandar."

"Incoming hail, Raas. From the lead Vandar warbird."

I waved a hand at the fuzzy screen. "Can we get it onscreen?"

The communications chief let loose a torrent of Vandar curses as he swiped at his console. Finally, a distorted view of Raas Kaalek filled the screen, as the image flickered.

The other Raas also appeared disheveled, and even with the grainy image, I could see that his command deck was damaged, as well.

"I know the attack did not come from your warbirds," Kaalek said, his expression menacing. "But did you lure our horde here? Are you working with the Zagrath?"

My mouth went dry. The Zagrath? "The enemy you defeated?"

Kaalek braced his hands on his hips as he glared through the screen. "Clearly, they have not all been beaten back."

I thought about what Sloane had told me about her personal mission and her beliefs that the empire hadn't been destroyed. She was convinced that they were regrouping somewhere and preparing to return with a vengeance. Maybe her suspicion wasn't so crazy after all.

I cleared my throat. "The female we took captive was on a mission to find hidden pockets of Zagrath forces when we intercepted her. She believes that the empire has forces that were not destroyed."

Kaalek rubbed a hand across his forehead, smearing blood on his skin like war paint. "It seems your prisoner was correct."

A sinking sensation churned in my gut. "Our presence must have alerted the Zagrath, and your horde's arrival must have been too good of an opportunity to miss. I swear on the gods of old that we did not intend to bring you into a battle with the empire."

Kaalek's grimace spread into a grin. "You have exposed Zagrath ships we did not destroy and imperial fighters who have not been punished for their deeds. There is nothing to regret. They were clever in making it appear as if we'd attacked each other, but their attempt to provoke us into a war against each other failed." Then his dark eyes flashed. "This will be the first test of our new alliance. Are you ready to show the Vandar what the Kyrie are made of?"

I growled, my lip curling. "For Vandar!"

Raas Kaalek drew his battle axe from where it was strapped to his back and thrust it into the air. "For Vandar!"

All the raiders on both ships jammed fists and axes high as they repeated the battle cry. "For Vandar!"

"Sending you new battle formation schematics on an encrypted channel," Kaalek said before he vanished from sight and the screen went black.

"Show me the enemy ships." My heart pounded as the lights pulsing blue changed to the deep purple we used when we went to battle.

Without a word, the communications chief swiped and tapped until the glass that stretched from one end of the command deck to the other was filled with the view of space—and of a fleet of hulking gray ships.

Excitement tingled up my spine as bursts of weapons fire erupted from the blackness and hurtled toward the Zagrath ships. The Vandar were attacking.

"Fire at will!" I shouted.

"All glory to Lokken," my majak said beside me.

"Glory to Lokken," I repeated, the mantra making my chest swell with pride. The Kyrie Vandar were fighting alongside the Vandar. Just as it had been intended. Just as we had desired.

My thoughts wandered to Sloane, regret hollowing my victory. I did not have *all* I desired.

CHAPTER
THIRTY-FOUR

Sloane

"The Zagrath?" The Vandar battle chief shook his head as he gaped at the view from the narrow slats of glass. "The empire the Vandar defeated?"

I frowned at him. "I keep telling everyone they weren't defeated. At least, not all of them." I flapped a hand at the gunmetal-gray ships. "See?"

Despite being proven right, the sight of the cruel imperial ships didn't bring me any satisfaction. My gut might have told me that the empire wouldn't have been so quickly dissipated, but deep down I'd hoped I was wrong. I could have happily gone the rest of my life without laying eyes on the brutal battleships again.

I shivered. It was as if they'd materialized from the shadows. Where had they even hidden such a large fleet? How had I missed this in all my searches? I wanted to kick myself for not having found them before they'd struck again.

"How is this possible?" The battle chief raked a hand through his pale hair. "How did they find us?"

I didn't have the answer to that, but I suspected that the arrival of the Kyrie Vandar and the encounter with the other Vandar horde had not gone unnoticed. I must have been on the right track with my hunt, since our current coordinates weren't far from where I was discovered. Had the Zagrath been lying in wait?

Another chill slid down my spine as I thought about what might have happened to me if it had been the empire who'd found me instead of Raas Ronnan. Thoughts of the Raas jerked me into action.

I spun to face the battle chief. "You need to go tell the Raas who's behind the attack. You'll need to join forces with the other Vandar if you're going to beat them—and the Valox, if they can get here fast enough."

He straightened and gave me a suspicious look. "Now you wish to help us? Where was this cooperation when we needed your help to find the Vandar?"

I huffed out an impatient breath as the ship shook again. I did not have time to rehash this crap. "I told you. Just because I'm part of the Valox rebellion doesn't mean I can call the Vandar whenever I want."

"Your friends did."

That was a good point. How had Cassie and Thea managed to get the Vandar horde to agree to a meeting? I had a lot to ask my friends when I saw them again—and a lot to tell. "They must have convinced the Valox leadership to make contact. I promise you that no mere pilot has the contacts to manage that."

He grunted, seeming to accept the logic of my statement. "You can tell the Raas yourself."

I hesitated as he waved me toward the door leading back to the main ship. Part of me wanted to see Ronnan again, but a bigger part of me knew he'd made his choice and it wasn't me. I couldn't be mad at him anymore. We'd both agreed that we couldn't be anything but a bit of fun. He'd never lied to me about using me for leverage, and even though it hurt when that was what he eventually did, I couldn't stay angry at the warlord for doing exactly what he'd originally said he'd do.

I shook my head firmly. "I'm of more use to you and the Vandar in the air."

His brows shot high as he darted a glance to the fighters that were being boarded by Vandar pilots, rocketing across the hangar bay, and shooting into space. "You wish to leave the warbird in a fighter?"

I narrowed my gaze at him. "I am a pilot, and I have more experience shooting Zagrath than you do."

He clenched his jaw. "The Raas will not like this."

"The Raas was sending me off the ship anyway. It's not like I'm escaping. Like you said, he was done with me. What does he care if I'm in a transport or in a fighter?"

"My task was to get you off the ship," he muttered. "And I have been counting the moments until the Raas is rid of the distraction of you."

I couldn't suppress a small smile that I'd been a distraction that had irritated the battle chief. If I didn't want to get the chance to blow more imperial fighters from the sky, I might have insisted on staying just to annoy the arrogant Vandar.

"This is a win for both of us," I told him as a group of kilted raiders pounded past us toward a vessel. "I get to do what I'm best at—shooting down Zagrath ships—and you get to say you did what you were asked to do—get me off the ship."

"Fine." He shot me a dark look even as he agreed. "But I cannot allow you to take a Vandar ship."

I put my hands on my waist and jutted out one hip. "Do you expect me to flap my way to the other ship?"

One corner of his mouth curled up in a half smile half grimace. I was sure he'd very much like to have me expelled from the ship without a vessel. "You can take your own ship."

"The one that was dead in the water when you found me?" I followed the warrior as he strode around several silver-hulled ships until we reached the end of the line—and my battle-scarred ship. Even with the scorch marks on the dingy hull, I stroked a hand fondly across the metal.

"We fixed it," he said gruffly. "And our engineers updated the technology and weaponry." He made a face that told me he hadn't supported this decision. "By order of the Raas."

My pulse quickened. "You souped-up my ship?"

His brow furrowed in confusion at my old Earth slang. It didn't matter. I smiled at him as I headed inside the ship. "Tell the Raas...thanks."

There was so much more I wanted to tell him, but I doubted my messenger could be relied on to convey long, heartfelt messages.

He grunted in response, inclining his head slightly. "I hope you destroy many enemy ships, human." Then he pivoted from me and strode purposefully from the hangar bay.

"So do I, Vandar," I said under my breath, as I made my way quickly into the cockpit and flopped into the pilot's seat.

I rubbed the console as I started to sing. "She was a fast machine, she kept her motor clean. She was the best damn woman that I ever seen." I fired up the engine, thrilling when it purred to life beneath me. "Let's go show these Vandar what a woman can do."

Then I gunned the ship, shot down the length of the hangar bay, and burst into space.

CHAPTER THIRTY-FIVE

Ronnan

I leaned to one side as the ship banked hard and dipped beneath a massive Zagrath battleship. The laser cannons mounted to the hull were firing rapidly, but we'd evaded them and were now firing up, our own lasers slicing into the dull-metal hull. We couldn't see what the other Vandar ships were doing since we were all using our invisibility shielding, but following the schematics sent over by Kaalek insured we wouldn't hit our fellow horde ships.

"This is even more successful than the amoeba pattern." One of our raiders pumped a fist into the air as another imperial ship exploded on our view screen.

"It's an enhanced version of the amoeba," Ayden said. "Meant for multiple hordes working in tandem."

"They must have developed them when they reunited." I thought about what Kaalek had told me about his Raas brothers. He understood being estranged and feeling adrift. I'd sensed it when he'd met my eyes. We were not so different, despite the many light years between our homes.

Even though we were embroiled in a violent battle, I couldn't help feeling a sense that we'd finally found what we'd craved for so long. Maybe it felt even more real since we were fighting side-by-side with our long-lost Vandar brothers. There was nothing so Vandar as bonding over a bloody battle.

Kaiven burst onto the command deck, breathing heavily. It was clear he'd raced through the ship to reach us.

"The Zagrath," he gasped. "They have not been destroyed as the Vandar believed."

"Yes, battle chief." I waved for him to stand with us and apprise the battle. "It was not the Vandar who attacked us, as we originally thought. Raas Kaalek was also attacked by the imperial forces."

Kaiven scowled as he took his place to one side of me. "They look even more gruesome from here."

"We are using the battle schematics sent to us by Raas Kaalek," Ayden told him, leaning forward to meet his gaze across me. "It is an augmented amoeba pattern designed for multiple hordes fighting in tandem."

"Multiple hordes," Kaiven whispered, awe evident in his tone.

"It is hard to believe that our mission has been successful," I said. "After so much uncertainty."

"The Vandar welcome us back? They restore our honor and the honor of our fathers?"

I didn't want to admit that I hadn't gotten to that part with Kaalek. "First, we battle together, as a test of our new alliance. Since we did not get to fulfill the original terms."

Kaiven shifted beside me.

I cut my gaze to him. "I know there was not time to return Sl... the female to the Vandar. We were attacked before the prisoner could be released."

"That is true, Raas. The female was not transported to the Vandar ship. We were hit before she could board the vessel."

I released a breath, finding myself more relieved than I wished to admit. I did not know what I intended to do now that Sloane was still on the ship, but my heart raced with the thought of her waiting for me in my quarters. My blood always ran hot after a battle, and I would not mind tangling with her to release some of tension of the day.

True, she'd been furious at me when I'd sent her away, but that had been before. Now that we were forming an alliance with the Vandar through battle, the return of our prisoner would not be so crucial. If she stayed on board a bit longer, would they care? Not after we'd fought together. Not when Raas Kaalek's warriors would be too busy celebrating our inevitable victory to concern themselves with the matter of a single female.

"If she was not transported to the Vandar," Ayden asked, "did she return to the Raas' quarters?"

I shot a curious glance at my *majak*. What a strange question. Where else would Kaiven have taken her? If he'd decided to bring her to the *oblek*, he would have had to traipse her through the command deck—and suffer my wrath.

My battle chief glared at Ayden. "She did not."

I swung my head to Kaiven. "Why not? If she wasn't transported from the warbird, where did you put her?"

He steeled his face, his gaze locked somewhere above my head. "I put her nowhere, Raas. She left."

A deadly rumble rose in my chest as my already rapid heart rate increased. "You speak to your Raas in riddles? You said she was not transported from our warbird."

"She was not. The female left on her own ship."

Ayden sucked in a breath, and Kaiven's belligerent expression faltered.

Anger pulsed through me at my battle chief's treachery, and I considered drawing my battle axe on him. But killing one of my officers in the middle of a battle would not inspire confidence among my raiders, especially if I lashed out because of a human female. A female I'd insisted all along was nothing more than a prisoner and a pawn.

I closed my eyes for a beat to temper my rage. When I opened them, I turned to fully face Kaiven, glaring at him until he met my gaze. "You thought it was wise to allow our only leverage against the Vandar to fly away during a battle with the Zagrath Empire?"

As I said the words, the reality of Sloane flying in the thick of the battle hit me. I pivoted to the view screen, a sick sense of failure swirling in my stomach.

"She insisted that she should be in the fight, Raas. She argued that she had more experience killing Zagrath than we did."

All of that was true, but it didn't mean I wanted her fighting by herself in her battered vessel. No matter how skilled a pilot she was, or how many improvements I'd had made to her ship, the battle was intense, with laser fire and photon torpedoes blasting from all sides.

"She begged to go," Kaiven said. "And she asked me to thank you."

My throat was thick. "That is all she said?"

He twitched one shoulder up. "I do not think she trusted me with more."

I allowed the anger to flow from me. She'd begged him to let her leave. Of course, she had. I gave her no reason to stay. No reason to want to see me ever again. Now she was gone, and I would never see her again, even if she survived the battle. My heart twisted painfully in my chest.

It didn't matter who won the battle anymore. I had already lost.

CHAPTER
THIRTY-SIX

Sloane

My hands buzzed with anticipation as I gripped the stick. I was flying manually again, which was the way I liked it. I preferred to fly by feel instead of instruments, even though few pilots relied on anything but technology anymore.

"That's why old school is better," I said to myself. "Whether it's music or piloting."

The other pilots in the rebellion might not agree, but that was fine. I'd never needed to go along with the crowd.

I banked abruptly to one side, skirting underneath a Zagrath ship before it could react. Once I'd cleared it, I did a hard reverse and flipped the ship, so I was facing the opposite direction and directly at the enemy ship.

"*Hasta la vista*, baby." I opened fire on them as I reversed from the explosion. Ancient Earth movies were also the best for kick-ass lines, no matter how much they annoyed my friends.

My heart raced as I quickly scanned the sky for another target. Despite the number of Zagrath vessels, it seemed like the Vandar were actually winning the fight. I couldn't see the warbirds, but they were effectively blasting fighter after imperial fighter from the sky. It was strange to have invisible allies, but I'd take it if it meant taking out these imperial insurgents.

"I knew I was right about them." I shook my head as I honed in on another Zagrath fighter. "No way an empire as obsessed with control wouldn't have a backup plan."

I wondered if this was the entirety of their reserve forces, but I suspected it wasn't. This was probably only a fraction of the ships and soldiers they were hiding as they rebuilt their army. The only reason they'd resurfaced before they were ready to reveal their full might was because the possibility of taking out two Vandar hordes was too tempting to ignore.

"Big mistake," I whispered, as I flew above my target and locked onto their engines. I fired a volley of crimson laser-fire at the ship, hoping the invisible Vandar ships knew to stay out of my way, and grinning when the enemy vessel blew. "Huge."

All around me, the sky glowed red and explosions illuminated the darkness like the ancient fireworks I'd seen in old vids. If it wasn't so violent, it would have been beautiful. Still, the middle of a battle was where I felt most comfortable, and defeating the enemy made satisfaction surge through me. It was almost enough to make me forget about my heartache over never seeing Ronnan again.

"It's done," I muttered fiercely. "It was never going to be anything real, anyway. It was just a fun distraction with a hot guy. Take it for what it was and move on to more important things, Sloane."

"How hot was he?"

I jerked at the voice surrounding me in the cockpit. "Thea?" I was somewhere between laughter, relief, and outrage. "Did you patch into my comms system?"

"Guilty," my friend said.

"I'm guilty too," Cassie's eager voice filled the cockpit. "We were just so excited to see your ship in the fight."

I steered my fighter to the outskirts of the battle to get a bird's-eye view, and so I wouldn't get shot down in my excitement to hear my friends' voices. "Are you in the fight?"

"What do you think?" Thea asked, as she appeared on my monitor.

"We were the ones who brought the Vandar horde to secure your release, so we were here when it all went down," Cassie added, waving at me over the vid link. "We didn't think the Vandar would release you this way, though."

"I kind of sweet-talked my way into the fight." I thought of the Vandar battle chief's reluctance to let me leave in my fighter, but also his eagerness to be rid of me. I wondered if Ronnan knew I was in the fight or if he believed me still to be on his ship. It didn't matter. He'd made it clear that I'd served my purpose and he was done with me.

"Does your sweet-talking have anything to do with the hot guy you were mumbling about when we hooked into your comms?" Cassie asked.

"Actually, no. The hot guy isn't anyone important." I rubbed the prickling skin at my neck. "What matters is that I'm no longer a prisoner of the Vandar, and that I'm back fighting the empire with my best friends."

"About that, Sloane." Thea cleared her throat. "It's safe to say you were right about the Zagrath. I'm sorry we didn't believe you."

"We should have had your back," Cassie said, her voice cracking.

"I don't blame you, although I think this proves that my gut is always right." It had been more than my gut, but I didn't want to rehash all my reasons for thinking the Zagrath were lying in wait.

"There'll be no living with you now." Thea rolled her eyes. "The Valox are on their way to join the fight, and you can bet that they're going to listen to you more after this."

I couldn't deny that I liked the idea of not being thought of as crazy or unable to let go of the war. Even the fighters who hadn't said anything to me directly, had clearly found my constant search missions bizarre.

"It's nice not to be thought of as crazy, but I'm not happy I was right about the empire." I sighed. "This means they're going to try to retake all the planets we've liberated."

"They can try." Thea let out a near growl. "But all those planets have tasted freedom. It's hard to extinguish a flame like that."

"And now we have even more Vandar to help in the fight." I scanned the sky, knowing the Vandar warbirds were flying unseen as lasers emerged from nothingness.

"You're going to have to tell us more about these new Vandar," Cassie said.

"After we kick some more Zagrath ass." Thea drew their ship up next to mine, and my two friends waved from their cockpit.

I waved back and then opened the neckline of my flight suit to scratch my burning skin. Had the Vandar washed my suit in Karillian fire ants?

"While you're filling us in on the new Vandar, you'll have to tell us about your new tattoo," Cassie said, her eyes squinting at me through the monitor.

I looked down at where I'd pulled open the fabric. Dark swirling lines were etched across my skin. My pulse quickened, and my eyelids burned as I stared at my skin. I had the exact same marks as Ronnan.

CHAPTER
THIRTY-SEVEN

Ronnan

My temples throbbed, as I stood rooted to the spot on my command deck. My gaze was trained on the battle raging around our warbird, but my mind wasn't on all the ships darting across the inky sky. It was on one ship.

Sloane was in the fray in her Valox fighter, a thought that made my stomach churn. I might have insisted her battered ship be repaired, and even updated with Vandar technology, but I hadn't allowed it to be outfitted with invisibility shielding. I hadn't anticipated her being in a raging battle against the Zagrath again, or I might have defied the Vandar rules about sharing our technological developments. Knowing she was facing off against imperial weaponry in an outdated Valox ship made me clench my jaw so tightly it ached.

"Do we have a lock on the Valox ship that left from our hangar bay?" I barked to Kaiven, as he stood hunched over a nearby console.

He glanced up at me. It hadn't been long since I'd first asked him to track Sloane's ship, and it was clear from his expression that my impatience wasn't helping. "Not yet, Raas."

"*Tvek.*" I cursed loudly, drawing stares from my crew. "How do we explain the prisoner we promised to deliver safely to the Vandar being killed in battle?"

There were murmurs of agreement even if there were some curious looks, including from my *majak* standing by my side.

"Raas Kaalek cannot blame us because the female insisted on leaving in her ship," he said, as our pilots skillfully maneuvered us through the volley of laser fire.

I released a breath. "No?"

"Is it the Raas's anger you fear, or your own?"

I cut my eyes to him briefly, all too aware that Ayden knew my heart better than anyone. "I made promises I did not keep."

He grunted, and I knew he was not fooled into thinking I meant promises made to Kaalek. "Vandar do not lie. Did you mean to keep these promises?"

I closed my eyes for a beat as I remembered the furtive words I'd whispered to Sloane when her naked body had been pressed to mine. I had not lied to the female. I'd meant every word I'd uttered to her, even if I'd had no right to utter them. "I did, but there is no place for my promises and our mission to coexist."

Ayden waved a hand at the wide stretch of glass overlooking the intense battle. "Our mission has already succeeded, Ronnan. We are fighting as brothers with Raas Kaalek and his horde. They have accepted us and welcomed us back into the fold. Isn't that what we wanted?"

I thought of my father's insistence on the Vandar bloodline. "It is not all."

Ayden scoffed. "We have already achieved more than our fathers did. Their desire for vengeance may have been our catalyst, but it does not have to define us anymore." He gripped my arm and turned to face me. "We are no longer the lost Vandar. We have done what our fathers could not or would not. We have reunited our horde with the hordes of our Vandar brothers. What we do next, and how we live our lives, is no longer defined by those who came before."

I allowed myself a shaky breath as I met my *majak's* gaze. There was a very good reason that Ayden was my most trusted advisor. He could see what I was blinded to by my determination to fulfill my role as Raas.

"The only reason you were not Raas is because you did not desire it," I told him.

"And because I am not the *pendayq* that you are." The edges off his lips quirked as if he hadn't just leveled a hardcore Selkee insult at me.

I choked back a laugh. "That would have earned anyone else time in the *oblek.*"

My *majak* shrugged. "I am not anyone else."

I pivoted back to the battle, my *majak's* words echoing in my head. He was right. I had done my duty as Raas. I had led my horde to Vandar space and negotiated our place within the Vandar empire. We were no longer exiled or forgotten. Did I owe it to my father to sacrifice even more?

I thought of my mother, who had not been Vandar. Had she been less brilliant or beautiful because of it? Had I loved her less because she wasn't Vandar? I growled at the treacherous thought, anger burning within me.

My love for my mother could not be tarnished because she was Selkee, just as my love for Sloane could not be denied because she was human. My heart stuttered in my chest. Was it possible I loved Sloane?

I gave my head a rough shake. I had become infatuated with her the more time we spent together and there was no doubt that she provoked my desire more than any female had, but love? The ache in my chest made my weak mental protestations crumble like stone beneath the heel of an iron boot.

"It is done, Raas."

I was jerked from my thoughts by my battle chief's booming voice. I spun toward him. "You found her?"

"We have located the Valox fighter that we repaired and enhanced."

My pulse tripped, but I tempered my excitement. "You are sure?"

"The Vandar enhancements we made to the ship made it possible to trace, Raas." He gave me an almost imperceptible nod. "It is her."

I swung my head back to the view screen. "Let me see."

Instantly, our view honed in on a small, ship that wasn't as shiny as the others. It was flying beside another Valox ship. Her rebel friends, I assumed.

For a moment, I considered leaving her. She had begged to leave and return to the fight. Maybe being with the Valox was where she belonged. Then I spotted the fleet of Zagrath fighters zeroing in on the two Valox ships.

"Target those imperial fighters," I yelled over my shoulder as I ran for the exit.

"Raas?" Kaiven called after me.

"You have command," my *majak* told him as he ran after me.

I glanced at Ayden as I raced toward the hangar bay. "You don't have to follow me, *majak*. What I'm doing is something you should be advising against."

"That's why I'm coming, Ronnan." A wicked grin spread across his face. "I cannot let you have all the fun."

CHAPTER
THIRTY-EIGHT

Sloane

"Another one bites the dust," I sang as I shot up another Zagrath ship. The influx of enemy fighters had meant that I'd had to distance myself from Cassie and Thea's ship, but almost as soon as the ships had arrived, the Vandar had picked them off one by one. I'd been able to finish off the last ones, but I owed the invisible horde a debt of gratitude.

I scanned the battle, searching for Cassie and Thea's ship, but it was hard to see through the explosions and red lasers slicing through the blackness. One thing I did notice was the reduction in the number of imperial fighters. Even the ones that were still zipping across the sky were heading toward the hulking gray battleships, and not toward the heart of the fighting.

"That's right, you bastards. Run away like the cowards you are!"

My chest swelled with pride. I was part of the reason their forces were depleted, and it felt good. Killing imperial soldiers made it easier to ignore the heat blooming across my chest and the marks etching themselves on my skin. I hadn't explained to my friends that it wasn't a tattoo they'd spotted. How did you tell someone that you'd gotten mating marks from a guy who'd dumped you?

I hadn't even known it was possible to get the Vandar marks if you weren't seriously attached—and I definitely wasn't. I scratched at my flesh, wishing the marks would disappear. The last thing I needed was a reminder of a guy who'd tossed me aside. I groaned. Maybe they'd fade once we were farther apart, or once I returned to my regular life and was far away from the Vandar.

"If not, I'm going to be wearing a lot of turtlenecks," I grumbled.

The blinking light on my console drew my attention, and I accepted the incoming transmission as I flipped my ship around and flew in an evasive pattern. "I'm surprised you didn't just patch into my comms system again, Thea."

"It is not Thea."

I twitched at the sound of Ronnan's distinctive voice, the velvet purr sending heat sizzling across my skin. "Oh." I tamped down the nervous flutter in my chest and made me voice emotionless. "What do you want?"

"It isn't safe for you out here. I'm coming to escort you to safety. *Vaes!*"

A laugh burst from me. "You came to get me, and you expect me to obey you? I'm not under your control anymore, Raas. And I thought we were done. You were fine with me leaving your ship earlier."

There was a heavy silence from the Raas. "I was hasty. I should not have let you leave."

"Because I can't take care of myself and you think I need a big, strong Vandar to babysit me?" The heat of desire that had danced down my spine had now morphed into anger. "I'll have you know I've been doing just fine out here by myself."

"I am still responsible for your safety," Ronnan growled. "I promised Raas Kaalek that the Valox would get their pilot back safely."

"Still trying to protect your pawn?" I shook my head, disgusted that I'd believed for a moment that this was about something more than Ronnan's precious mission. "Well, you don't have to worry about that. I've been fighting with my Valox friends, and they'll tell the Vandar that you released me. You got what you needed from me, right?"

There was more silence.

"Thanks for fixing up my ship, by the way. It hasn't flown this fast in ages." To prove that, I gunned the engine and stopped on a dime, flipping my ship over so that I was facing the other direction, and was nose-to-nose with his ship, which had been behind me. Even through the glass of his cockpit, I could see the stern expression on his face.

"You are welcome." He let out a heavy breath. "Sloane—"

"I'd love to hang out and chat, but I just saw Cassie and Thea." My stomach lurched as I spotted a group of Zagrath fighters surrounding them. "Gotta go save their asses!"

I disconnected our transmission, flipped my ship again, and flew through the battle toward the other Valox fighter. The imperial fighters were chasing them in an attack formation. My friends were doing a good job of evading them, but they were outnumbered. I zoomed in from behind, blasting the two fighters in the rear and sending them both spiraling off with their engines burning.

"Miss me?" I asked, as the comms connection crackled to life.

Thea's rumbly laugh engulfed me. "You could say that. Thanks for the save."

"Anytime." I clocked a massive Zagrath battleship a bit too close for comfort. "How about we bug out of here?"

"Yes, please," Cassie's voice was more high-pitched, which told me she was more nervous than usual.

I flew alongside my friends' ship, waving at them. Then my ship jolted, as if I'd flown into a wall. What the hell? My console showed no impact or malfunction. I glanced back over at Cassie and Thea. Both of their eyes were wide as their ship lurched.

It only took me a heartbeat to realize that we were both being pulled into the Zagrath ship.

"You wanted to find the Zagrath," Thea said dryly, as our ships were tractored toward the gray vessel.

"I take it back," I rubbed my sweaty palms on the front of my flight suit as I thought of what I'd heard happened to rebels taken captive by the empire. Then I scratched the prickling skin on my chest and thought of Ronnan and how cold I'd been to him. "I take it all back."

THIRTY-NINE

Ronnan

My conversation with Sloane had not gone how I'd intended. No surprise that she hadn't been receptive to my attempts to remove her from the battle, but I hadn't expected her to so easily dismiss me. Her accusations that I'd had no issue letting her go when she was on the ship had stung, but she hadn't been wrong in thinking that. She'd only seen what I wanted her and my Vandar raiders to see—a strong Raas who was not influenced by a female. The truth was anything but that.

"Raas?" My *majak's* voice prodded me back to the reality of being beside him in the cockpit of a raiding vessel in the midst of a battle.

"She is right. The Vandar will know we released her in good faith." I huffed out an irritated breath. "I cannot force her to do anything anymore."

"Return to the horde?"

I clenched my jaw, resisting leaving Sloane unprotected. Protection she did not want, I reminded myself. I would have to accept that she no longer needed me—or wanted me.

Before I could agree to return to our warbird, I spotted Sloane's ship taking out a pair of fighters that had been chasing her friends' ship. *Tvek*, she was as good a pilot as she'd claimed. Part of me wished to stay in the battle just to watch her artfully maneuver her ship but watching her would only make the regret inside me grow.

Where would I find a female who would challenge me the way she had? Would a Vandar female be as knowledgeable about battle strategy? Would they be able to beat me at Zindar?

It took me a moment to register Sloane's ship becoming immobilized. I peered through the laser fire at the pair of Valox fighters, cursing when I realized that they'd both been caught in a tractor beam from the nearby Zagrath battleship.

"The imperial battleship is dragging the Valox ships inside," I said, as I punched in an intercept course.

Ayden cut a glance to me. "What can we do, Raas?"

My first instinct was to order the hordes to destroy the Zagrath vessel, but Sloane's ship was too close. It would be incinerated in any explosion big enough to take out a battleship. The tractor beam itself was too strong to break and getting near it would mean being pulled in as well.

I emitted a growl as I considered our options. "We are in a raiding vessel."

My *majak* glanced over his shoulder at where a team of raiders would normally stand, waiting to rush onto an enemy ship with axes drawn. "With no raiders."

"We do not need a team to extract a few humans." I revised our heading to approach the underbelly of the imperial ship. "All we need are our raiding clamps." I touched a hand to the hilt of my weapon. "And our axes."

"Your plan, Raas?"

"We cannot allow the empire to take the Valox females." The thought of the sworn enemy of the Vandar laying a finger on Sloane turned my stomach. "They are resistance fighters. If the Zagrath wish to break the resistance, it makes sense that they will try to extract information from its fighters."

Ayden made a low sound in his throat, voicing both his disapproval of the Zagrath and his distaste for what they might do to Sloane and her friends.

"We will board the ship as if we were raiders, find the females, and take them from the ship," I said as I instigated our invisibility shielding.

"I do not wish to question your strategy, Ronnan, but how will we move around a Zagrath ship without being noticed?" He flicked a hand at our bare chests and battle kilts. "From what I understand, the imperial soldiers wear significantly more clothing than we do."

I slid my gaze to the leather strips parting to reveal my thick thighs. My *majak* had a point. We were not overpowering the Zagrath with our raiders. As only two Vandar, we would need to rely on stealth and cunning more than brute force. "We will adapt our plan once onboard the vessel." I glanced at my axe. "Blood might flow."

Ayden nodded, as we flew closer to the hulking gray vessel. Neither of us were a stranger to violence or bloodshed. If it was needed to save Sloane and her friends, we would not hesitate.

Our ship skirted underneath the enemy ship, and I found a vertical protrusion. Then I used our raiding clamps to secure us to the hull and cut a hole through the thick steel.

With our own ship's controls locked, Ayden and I took up positions and prepared to board the vessel.

I stole a glance at him as the final cut was burned into the hull, and the scent of scorching steel filled the air. "For Vandar."

He met my gaze with a fierce one of his own, reminding me that he was still a highly trained Vandar warrior with a thirst for battle. "For Vandar!"

I led us onto the ship, quickly assessing where we were, which was exactly where I'd hoped we'd be—in the lower storage area along with stacks of crates and rows of iron barrels. Our raiding clamps emitted power signatures that muddled sensors, so even if our presence was detected, the Zagrath wouldn't be able to determine that their hull had been breached. I was counting on fluctuations in a remote storage area during a battle being ignored.

"*Vaes.*" My skin tingled as I held my axe in both hands and motioned with a jerk of my head for Ayden to follow me down a corridor.

When we rounded the corner, we stopped short as we almost ran headlong into a pair of Zagrath soldiers. They were beefy males who appeared to be guards, but they hadn't been expecting us. Without pausing to think about it, I knocked one out with the flat of my blade then flipped it around and whacked the other with the heavy handle as he turned to run. Both collapsed in heaps on the floor.

"You didn't kill them," Ayden noted as I bent down.

I scratched at my chest, the tingling sensation I'd felt moments earlier now an uncomfortable burning. I started to remove the dark uniform from one of the unconscious males. "We need their uniforms, and I didn't want to be covered in their blood."

My *majak* stared at me, his eyes widening.

"You have a problem disguising ourselves as the enemy?"

He shook his head. "No, *majak*."

I noticed that his eyes were fixed on my chest where I'd been scratching. I peered at my own flesh, and my heart lurched. My mating marks were extending up my neck and down my shoulders.

"You have found your true mate, Raas," he whispered almost reverently.

I'd found her, and I'd pushed her away and into the clutches of the enemy.

CHAPTER
FORTY

Sloane

"You don't need to shove," I grumbled, as an imperial soldier propelled me from my ship and into the vast hangar bay of the Zagrath battleship. I didn't want to gape, but it was hard not to stare at the soaring ceiling criss-crossed with gleaming chrome beams. Staircases hugged the walls, with dark-uniformed soldiers clomping up and down them. Unlike the hangar bay at the Valox base, the floors here were shiny, despite the number of boots I assumed goose-stepped across it on the regular.

Part of me was shocked that the empire had been able to hide battleships of this magnitude and staff them with enough remaining imperial soldiers, while another part of me wasn't at all surprised that the galactic empire which had controlled the galaxy for generations had been able to rebuild itself enough to strike back so swiftly after its demise. Still, my gut twisted at the reality of the return of the empire.

"Where do you want this one?" The solider jamming a blaster in my back asked, as he approached a straight-backed officer peering at an electronic tablet.

Without glancing up, the Zagrath waved a hand. "Put her in the brig with the other ones. Someone will get them for interrogation soon."

I swallowed hard when I heard the word interrogation. I hoped I'd be tough enough not to crack under whatever brutal techniques they planned to use.

My fears were momentarily forgotten when I was shoved toward two familiar figures. I had to suppress the urge to squeal and throw my arms around Thea and Cassie, when I saw them between a pair of grim-faced soldiers. Thea's black braid fell down her back, which was ramrod straight, while Cassie flicked her blue hair from her face nervously.

My chest swelled with affection for the friends who'd come looking for me and even brought a Vandar horde to secure my freedom. Then I remembered that we were all headed for interrogation.

"Sorry I got you into this," I said in a low voice once we were pushed together.

"It's not your fault," Cassie assured me, darting an arm around my shoulders and squeezing before the soldiers could notice. "You didn't know the Zagrath would appear."

"Maybe she did." Thea gave me a nod. "And maybe if we and the rest of the resistance had listened to her earlier, we wouldn't be in this situation."

"You couldn't have known," I said. "I didn't *know*. I just had a hunch."

"A hunch that was right." Thea gave me a small smile. "I'm sorry I didn't take you more seriously."

My throat tightened. "Hey, stop that. You two came after me and brought a Vandar horde."

Cassie jerked a thumb at Thea. "Apparently, this girl made friends with the wife of a Raas."

I cocked an eyebrow at our friend. "One of the human ones?"

Thea nodded as the Zagrath soldiers poked us in the back to move forward. "Tara, Raas Kaalek's wife or mate or whatever."

"Wouldn't she be called Raisa?" Cassie asked, lowering her voice, since we were between two pairs of imperial soldiers as we were marched through the hangar bay.

Thea twitched one shoulder. "She just goes by Tara. She's pretty laid back about the whole Vandar thing, although I get the feeling that it fits in with her personality." Her gaze dropped to my throat. "That's funny. Her mating marks look a lot like your new tattoo."

Cassie almost tripped over her own feet as she swiveled her head to stare at my chest, which I reflexively scratched. "When would you have gotten a tattoo? You didn't have it when you left the Valox base."

I blew out a breath, stealing a glance in front of us and behind to be sure the soldiers weren't listening, but they were too busy talking to each other to care about what some human prisoners were saying. "It's not exactly a tattoo."

We were led from the wide opening to the hangar bay and down a long corridor with impossibly shiny metal walls, and floors that echoed every sharp footfall. I was grateful for the sound to mask my confession.

"I think these are Vandar mating marks."

Both of my friends stared at me with open mouths.

"Vandar mating marks?" Cassie repeated, brushing her hair from her face with her fingers. "I thought only the Vandar's true mates could get those? Isn't it really unusual that the humans who became the mates of the warlord brothers got them?"

I shrugged. "No idea. I don't know much about mating marks, but I don't know what else this could be." I raked my fingers across my neck. "It burns like crazy."

Thea pinned me with a serious look. "Does this mean you got involved with one of the Vandar while you were their prisoner?"

We turned down a narrower and dimmer corridor, and more Zagrath soldiers fell in step behind us. It seemed like we were going deeper into the ship, which was where I suspected their brig and interrogation rooms were kept.

"Of course, she did," Cassie said before I could speak, flapping a hand at my throat. "You don't get branded by the Vandar without forming some sort of connection or bond." She focused on my marked skin and let out a low whistle. "A pretty intense bond from the look of those marks."

Thoughts of Ronnan made my eyes sting with tears, but I blinked them away, refusing to shed any tears for him. "Whatever I had with the Raas—however intense it might have felt at the time—is over. As soon as he had the chance to return me, he did."

"Did you say Raas?" Thea's voice was so soft I almost missed her question.

I didn't miss the same question barked from one of the soldiers behind me. "Did you say Raas?"

We all stiffened as all the Zagrath stopped walking and spun on me. Even the imperial soldiers walking behind our group paused to watch what was happening. I tried to back away but the soldier who'd spoken grabbed my collar and ripped it open.

I yelped as my chest was bared, but the Zagrath weren't looking at my bra or my cleavage. They were looking in horror at the mating marks blooming across my flesh.

Then one of them gave me a cruel smile, taking hold of one side of my collar and jerking me to him. "Looks like we captured a Vandar's whore."

Cassie and Thea both came to my defense, yelling at the soldier to let me go as I kicked out at him. But it was an entirely different voice—deep, velvety, and menacing—that froze everyone in their tracks.

"She is no one's whore. Remove your hands from my mate before I tear them from your body."

CHAPTER
FORTY-ONE

Ronnan

Our luck had almost been too good to believe as we'd made our way up from the bowels of the battleship and found ourselves falling in step behind the imperial guards surrounding Sloane and her friends. Ayden shot me a look as we trailed them, but the soldiers were too busy talking to each other to pay attention to a pair of similarly-uniformed soldiers like us.

If they'd bothered to look closer, they might have noticed that the fabric of the uniforms was pulled taut over our muscles, and the pants barely reached the tops of our lace-up boots. We'd had to tuck our tails down one leg of the pants, making them even less comfortable, and jam our hair under flat-topped hats. Even with all our adjustments, we did not look like the clean-shaven Zagrath, with closely cropped hair and no weapons, save blasters attached to their waists. We'd kept the blasters that had belonged to the soldiers we'd left tied up in a dimly lit hallways, but I'd insisted on bringing our battle axes, so we held them behind our legs as we walked.

I exchanged a look of surprise when our presence didn't even warrant a second glance from the guards tasked with escorting their Valox prisoners, and my *majak* and I both relaxed our grips on our axes. It would be better if we waited until we were farther away from the heart of the ship, and closer to where we'd entered the vessel.

My ears pricked when I heard the females mumbling about mating marks. Vandar mating marks? I caught Ayden stealing a questioning glance at me. He'd been the one to point out the marks that were currently being seared into my flesh, and now Sloane and her friends were discussing them?

My pulse spiked. Could it be possible that I wasn't the only one being affected? The thought of my marks on Sloane's skin sent a possessive thrill through me, and my cock twitched to life, reminding me painfully how tight the Zagrath pants were.

"Did you say Raas?" The imperial soldier stopped so quickly that Ayden and I almost plowed into the back of the group.

I adjusted my grip on my axe handle, rage making me see a red haze as the Zagrath ripped open Sloane's uniform top.

"Looks like we captured a Vandar's whore," he said, after he snatched her up by her collar.

Both of the other Valox females began shouting at the soldier, as Sloane tried to free herself from his grasp, but Ayden and I assumed battle stances, with our axes poised in front of us to strike.

"She is no one's whore. Remove your hands from my mate before I tear them from your body," I growled, my voice so low and venomous that even my *majak* twitched beside me.

The Zagrath whirled around, their mouths agape as we sprang into action, slicing down the two closest to us before they could fumble for their blasters. Sloane's friends dodged to the side, the taller female with brown skin snatching a blaster in the confusion and firing at one of the remaining soldiers. Sloane kneed the last Zagrath hard in the balls, staggering back as he doubled over and leaving enough space for me to swing my axe. The blade whizzed through the air, singing as it lopped off his head, which spun like a Dervian top before splatting to the floor.

When all the imperial bodies lay lifeless around us, Ayden and I straightened.

"Are you hurt?" He lowered his axe and stepped forward.

Thea and Cassie hadn't lost the stunned looks on their faces, but it was Sloane who stared at me like I was a spirit who had returned from Zedna.

"Ronnan?" Her voice broke as she touched a hand to her neck.

My gaze locked on the inky swirls etched on her chest. The sizzling on my own chest gave way to an impossible tightness. "You have my marks."

Ayden and the Valox women shifted and eyed us, all wordlessly stepping over the bodies and moving away.

Sloane nodded, biting the edge of her bottom lip and finally lifting her eyes to meet mine. "I didn't think it was possible." Then she dropped her gaze and shook her head. "I know what you said. I know you have to take a Vandar mate. I swear I didn't do this on—"

"I do not want a Vandar mate," I said loudly, cutting off her apologies. It pained me that she believed I could still want anyone but her after our connection had literally branded Vandar marking on her flesh.

She blinked at me, her brows knitting in confusion. "But you told me you had to take a Vandar mate or your mission was ruined. You returned me to the Valox without a second thought." Her eyes shone. "You made it clear that we were just a bit of fun, and you were done with me."

I leapt over the bodies between us, standing so close to her I could feel her ragged breath. "I was wrong—about all of it. I tried to deny what I felt for you because I wasn't supposed to feel those things, but I couldn't. I despised myself for letting you go. When I discovered you'd left the ship in your fighter, I couldn't bear the idea of you being in the battle and not being able to protect you."

"Why didn't you say that when you found my fighter?"

My heart thundered against my ribs as I brushed a single tear from her cheek. "You seemed in your element. I thought you would be happier returning to your Valox resistance." I touched a hand to the marks scorching my neck, and then to her marks, her usually cool skin burning with heat. "I didn't know about these."

"What does it mean?" Her voice quivered as her gaze went to my hand.

"It means that you are my true mate, and it means that my body knows what I've been too stubborn to admit."

Sloane hitched in a breath. "Even if I'm human?"

I shrugged. "I am not the first Vandar to fall in love with a human."

There were muffled gasps behind us, but Sloane didn't break eye contact, her pupils flaring. "Did you say...?"

"That I love you? I did." I wrapped an arm around her waist and pulled her flush to me. "Now *vaes*, female."

Her lips trembled into a smile. "Just because I love you too doesn't mean I'm going to obey everything you say."

My heart seemed to stop as I allowed her words to sink in. I returned her smile, cocking my head. "No?"

"No." She assumed an expression of mock seriousness. "Only the naughty orders, Raas."

I growled as I crushed my mouth to hers, savoring the taste I thought had been lost to me forever. Sloane sank into me, moaning softly, until Ayden's urgent tone pulled me from my euphoric daze.

"Raas," he said, as the sound of pounding boots approached. "I think it is time for us to go."

CHAPTER
FORTY-TWO

Sloane

I pulled back from Ronnan, panting a bit as I gazed up at him. I was still reeling from him being on the enemy ship, being oddly dressed in imperial clothing, and telling me that he loved me. Even so, I forced myself to focus on the sound of thudding footsteps approaching. None of the Raas' sweet words and heroic acts would mean much, if we were killed by the Zagrath. "I think your first mate is right."

"*Majak*," the Vandar said under his breath, as he shot furtive glances at Ronnan and then behind him.

"I'm with Majak." Cassie jerked a thumb toward him. "I think the Zagrath heard the blaster fire."

"I'm assuming you two have an escape plan?" Thea asked, snagging the blasters from the dead bodies strewn on the floor. She tossed one to me.

Ronnan grabbed my hand and tugged me forward. "Our raiding ship is hooked to the ship's hull, but we must continue deeper into the vessel."

Thea tossed a blaster to Cassie. "We're right behind you!"

Ronnan led the way, running with me by his side, while the other Vandar kept pace with Cassie and Thea. We hurried down a series of corridors, avoiding ones filled with soldiers, but the sounds of pursuit didn't fade.

We raced around one corner, and Ronnan skidded to a stop in the face of a group of imperial soldiers lying in wait with blasters drawn. He sliced his axe through the air to deflect the blaster fire, which ricocheted off the curved steel and scorched the ceiling and walls. I stifled a scream as he thrust me behind him and backed us quickly from the corridor.

"We can't go that way," he said, grasping my hand tighter and cutting his gaze to two diverging hallways. He locked eyes with his *majak*. "We should split up. You take the females to the ship, and I will draw the enemy fire away from you."

I shook my head. "I'm not leaving you."

"Stubborn female," he growled, but his scowl twitched into a half smile. "Then this is one of those occasions where you will have to obey me."

"How will you get to the ship?" Thea asked as Ronnan's *majak* motioned for her and Cassie to follow him.

"There are lots of ships around here." I winked at her. "I am a pilot, after all."

"Be safe," Cassie called out, her expression pained as she fell in step with Thea and the other Vandar down a narrower corridor.

I held out my blaster and pivoted back to the imperial soldiers. "Ready to be a distraction?"

With a rough grunt, Ronnan dropped my hand and snatched a blaster from the waistband of the snug, imperial pants. With his other hand, he gripped the handle of his axe. "I am ready to spill more imperial blood."

Before we could surge forward, the soldiers rounded the corner, but Ronnan and I both ducked as we unleashed our blasters. He used the broad blade of his axe as a shield as we backed up and fired over it.

The imperial soldiers were just as bad shots as they'd always been, and I wondered if they bothered training them at all. Then again, the Zagrath rarely engaged in hand-to-hand combat, since their method of control was to subdue through intimidation and economic strangleholds. One after another fighter dropped as we avoided their blaster fire, rising above Ronnan's axe just long enough to take our shots.

When there was one lone Zagrath remaining, Ronnan straightened and lunged for him, knocking his weapon from his hand. The soldier cowered as Ronnan heaved his axe up to render the final blow.

"Wait!"

He paused with the brutal weapon above his head, dragging in breath.

"I have a better idea for this one," I said, leveling my blaster at him. "He's going to lead us through this ship."

Ronnan slowly dropped his axe. "I would prefer to kill him."

"She's right." The Zagrath's hands shook as he held them up. "You won't be able to find your way out without someone who knows the layout of the battleship."

A dark rumble reverberated in Ronnan's chest as he eyed me. "You are very bad at obeying."

I grinned at him. "You haven't given me an irresistible order yet."

He huffed out a breath, sliding his hard gaze to the enemy soldier. "We need to get to the bottom of the ship where you store excess equipment and supplies."

The Zagrath straightened the crooked hat on his head as he shook it. "You don't want to go down there. That's where the others are searching."

"Searching?" Ronnan stepped closer to the fighter.

The man shrunk as the Vandar towered over him. "Sensors detected something unusual in that area. Our commander sent troops to investigate. Belowdecks is crawling with soldiers."

A muscle in Ronnan's jaw ticked as he clenched it.

I rested a hand on his arm. "Like I told Thea, there are other ways off this ship." I turned to the Zagrath. "Can you get us to the hangar bay?"

His brow furrowed as he nodded his head. "Yes, but that's not the best way to avoid being seen."

"It doesn't matter if we're seen." I eyed Ronnan again, hoping his ill-fitting uniform would be convincing enough. "Not when two soldiers are escorting a Valox prisoner."

Ronnan's frown deepened but I ignored him, pinning my gaze on the nervous solider. "You get us to my ship, and then you're free to go."

He gulped audibly, stealing a look to Ronnan. "You won't kill me."

Ronnan growled again. "If you tell the soldiers searching the lower decks to call off their search. Tell them you've found the intruders. Then I will consider allowing you to live."

I shot him a quelling glance. "I give you my word that we won't kill you. As long as you do what he says and don't betray us, I won't let the Vandar warlord rip off your arms."

Ronnan ran one finger along the bloody edge of his blade as the Zagrath soldier emitted a tiny squeak. "One more thing I dislike about this plan."

FORTY-THREE

Ronnan

I held Sloane's arm, marching her forward alongside the Zagrath and into the enemy's hangar bay. So far, the soldier had kept his part of the bargain. He'd brought us through the most deserted parts of the battleship and through secret passageways so that we'd barely encountered another soul. Still, standing alongside the sworn enemy of the Vandar sent waves of revulsion through me, and I was counting the moments until I could return to slaying my enemy instead of allying with him.

The hangar bay buzzed with activity as we entered. So many soldiers were running to ships or banging away on damaged ones that we were able to skirt around the sides of the massive space unnoticed.

"Almost there," Sloane muttered as her Valox fighter came into view. It was easily the oldest and most battered vessel on the deck, but I would take it any day over the Zagrath ships—especially since I knew of all the Vandar modifications I'd had made to it.

My thoughts went briefly to Ayden. He'd taken the Valox females to our waiting ship, but he'd had to lead them through the soldiers searching for the reason their sensors had been alerted. They might not be able to see our raiding vessel, but they would notice a hole in their hull connecting it to them. I could only hope that the barrels and crates we'd stacked in front would make it harder to find.

If anyone could fight his way through a bunch of Zagrath, it was my *majak*. He might not be fueled by an impulsive rage like me, but he was strategic and clever. He would be able to outthink any brainless imperial automaton. Besides, the Valox females seemed capable, and the one with dark hair had a ferocious streak to her.

"Is this your ship?" The imperial soldier's question snapped me from my worries.

I eyed the dented hull of the Valox ship, releasing a sigh of relief that it was not being guarded, or worse, disassembled for scrap.

"That's it," Sloane said from the corner of her mouth. She increased her pace, no doubt eager to get to the ship. We were so close.

"You there!" The deep bellowing voice made my stomach sink. "With the prisoner. Where are you taking her?"

We were only steps away from the ship, and the ramp was still down. The Zagrath with us gave me a hesitant glance as I slid the handle of my axe from where I'd hidden it up the length of my sleeve.

"I said," the imperial officer raised his voice as he strode closer, "where are you—?"

"I heard you the first time," I said through gritted teeth, as I spun around and swung my axe up, cracking his chin open and sending him flying back.

"So much for a clean getaway." Sloane dashed the last few steps to the ship and up the ramp.

The Zagrath soldier who'd escorted us through the ship swiveled his head to me, his eyes wide, as if expecting me to strike him down.

"A Vandar doesn't lie," I told him. "Go!"

He didn't wait, before turning and running through the soldiers who were starting to rush toward the commotion and gather around the bloody soldier on the floor. I raced onto the Valox ship as Sloane raised the ramp. She'd already powered up the engines and was strapped into the pilot's seat.

"Glad you could join me," she called over her shoulder, as I sank into the seat next to her. "Now get ready to hang on."

Without another word, she thrust us forward. We rocketed across the floor of the hangar bay, passing startled Zagrath, and exploding through the energy field and into space. The battle had slowed, and there were considerably fewer imperial fighters. Sloane didn't steer us through the battle, though. She hugged the hull of the ship, dipping beneath it.

"You said your raiding ship was attached to the underbelly of the battleship?"

I nodded. "It's using invisibility shielding. You won't be able to detect it."

She cursed. "How will we know that your *majak* and my friends got away?"

"Ayden will not fail." I felt this statement with every fiber of my being. My *majak* would get the females off the enemy ship.

Sloane pressed her lips together and nodded, before breaking off her flight around the hull. She zipped through the criss-crossing laser fire, putting distance between us and the Zagrath battleship, and flying evasively to avoid any ships that might have followed us.

"Where to?" she asked, once we'd deftly flown through the battle.

I sent an encrypted message to Kaiven, requesting coordinates, which I then entered into the Valox navigation system, which was now more like a Vandar navigational system. It wasn't until we touched down on the Vandar warbird, that I was able to breathe freely.

Kaiven met us at the bottom of the ramp, clicking his heels at me. "Welcome home, Raas." He glanced at the opening in the fighter, as if waiting for my *majak* to emerge.

"Ayden took the other Valox females and escaped in our raiding ship. He will be returning soon."

My battle chief nodded, as if he, too, knew this to be true.

"The battle?" I asked.

"The Zagrath are in retreat, Raas. The Valox fleet arrived, and the enemy ships have begun to depart." A grin split his face. "It is done. They are done." He slid his gaze to Sloane beside me. "I was right to let you join the battle, human."

I hadn't reconciled to my battle chief allowing Sloane to leave in her Valox ship, but he was right. She was a formidable pilot, even if I hated the thought of her being in danger.

"Let us not make it a habit," I said, giving them both severe looks.

Kaiven inclined his head at me, but I caught Sloane winking at him, which made him shift from one foot to the other and clear his throat.

I grabbed Sloane's hand and pulled her behind me, calling back to my battle chief. "Alert me the moment Ayden returns. I will be in my quarters."

"We aren't going to wait for them?"

My heart thundered as loud as my thudding boots as we passed raiders clicking their heels and exchanging knowing glances. "There is a saying on Selkee about a watched spring boiling." I leapt onto one of the fast-moving lifts and pulled her with me.

Sloane buried her face in my chest as we rose into the air. "There's an Earth saying like that too, but..."

I jumped off the continually moving lift and led her to the arched doorway to my quarters. "Our presence will not hasten their return." I waved a hand and the doors slid open. My *majak* will bring them back. Until then, there are preparations to be discussed for your Raisa ceremony."

"My...?" She gaped at me, as I led her across the glossy floor toward the bed. "Raisa?"

I stopped at the foot of the round bed and began to peel off her flight suit, while she stood immobilized, her eyes wide. "You thought we would share mating marks and I would not make you my Raisa?"

Her flight suit fell to a pool around her feet. "I didn't...I mean, I thought...I wouldn't want to assume..."

I put a finger to her lips. "You are mine, Sloane. These marks only prove what my heart already knew." My hands skimmed the sides of her body and settled on her hips, my tail coiling around the inside of one of her legs and provoking a shiver. "You will do me the honor of becoming my Raisa, and my mate for life."

She hitched in an uneven breath. "Are you asking or telling?"

I brushed my lips across hers "Consider this an order from your Raas."

She lifted her hands and fisted them into my hair, emitting her own low growl. "Yes, Raas."

Then I crushed my mouth to hers and we fell onto the bed together in a tangle of moans and writhing limbs.

CHAPTER
FORTY-FOUR

Sloane

Ronnan nuzzled my neck as he cupped my breasts from behind. The warm water cascaded from overhead and spilled over both of us, splashing on the slick, obsidian stone. I hadn't paid much attention to the shadowy side of the bathing chamber, but now that I was surrounded by water that flowed from above, but also from the side, and even from below, I realized how underrated it was.

"What happened to discussing my Raisa ceremony?" I asked, tipping my head back and releasing a breathy sigh.

"Well, first I had to claim you as my mate, and now I'm cleaning you." His hands roamed down my body, just as they had when he'd fucked me in his bed, and again in the bathing pools.

"Is that what you're doing?" I splayed one hand on the slippery stone wall for balance as his fingers continued to wander. As sore as I was, I couldn't seem to get enough of Ronnan. It had been deliciously forbidden when he was the Raas I could never fall for, but now that he was my mate for life, there was something even more intoxicating about submitting to him.

"Mmmm." He hummed a vague sound. "And now I need to taste you."

I rolled my head back and let the rushing water splash my face as he walked me over to a ledge inset in the stone that I hadn't noticed. He hoisted me up so I was perched on it, the water still hitting his back. I was too dazed to do much else but let my legs fall open as he knelt in front of me and hooked my knees over his shoulders.

If I'd thought the water was warm, the tongue that parted me was so hot it made me draw in a sharp breath. Ronnan slid it through me, delving inside me for a beat before continuing until he found my clit. I was already swollen and sensitive from my earlier orgasms, but his wet tongue caressed me so gently that I rocked my hips into him.

Even though I'd come twice already, I was hungry for more. I tangled my fingers in his wet hair and held his head between my legs as he softly sucked my clit. His fingers teased my opening, and I arched my back in anticipation of being filled by his fingers, but it was the wet fur of his tail that pushed inside me.

I gasped as his tongue swirled, and his tail stroked deep. I wrapped my legs tighter around him needing more. There was something so deliciously naughty about having the Vandar's tail fucking me that it sent ripples of pleasure through me one after the other as I screamed, my cries bouncing off the walls of the bathing chamber.

Almost as soon as my screams had faded, Ronnan stood and jerked my ass to the edge of the ledge, his tail pulling out as he thrust his cock inside me. "My tail prepared you for me, but this is what you want, isn't it?"

I bobbed my head as I gripped his slick shoulders.

"I can't get enough of you," he growled. "And now I never need give you up, do I? You're mine for life."

I moaned.

"Tell me who you belong to, Sloane," he commanded.

"I'm yours, Raas."

He pulled out and stared down at where my legs were spread for him, a dark rumble burgeoning in his throat. "Who does your pretty pussy belong to?"

"It's yours," I said as he thrust into me hard, and my breath left me.

He ran his hand up my neck until he was clutching my jaw. "Such a perfect Raisa who takes me like she was made for my cock—and my tail."

His mouth crashed onto mine, our moans mingling as he thrust into me, and our bodies slapped together. With a roar that was swallowed by our kiss, he pulsed hot into me. When he finally tore his mouth from mine, we were both panting.

"Raas?" The voice echoed off the dark stone and made Ronnan's breathing still as he held himself inside me.

"Kaiven," Ronnan murmured in my ear. "I told him to come tell me as soon as my *majak* returned."

My already fluttery pulse jumped. They were back!

"Has Ayden returned with the Valox females?" Ronnan called out as his battle chief remained outside the arched doorway.

"He has returned." Kaiven hesitated.

Ronnan stiffened, and my heart lurched with dread, the flutter of pleasure quickly replaced by the nervous patter of fear.

"What are you not telling me?" the Raas asked his battle chief, who did not reply.

CHAPTER

FORTY-FIVE

Ronnan

I strode onto the hangar bay, my damp hair dripping down my bare back. There had been no time to do more than leap from the bathing pool and throw on my battle kilt and boots. Not after my battle chief had given me the news.

"What do you mean the ship barely made it?" I growled at Kaiven, flicking my gaze to my side as he kept pace with me.

"But they did make it?" Sloane asked, peering at Kaiven from the other side of me as she almost jogged to keep up with us. Her hair was also wet and leaving a trail of water droplets behind us and down the back of the wrinkled flight suit she'd thrown on. "All of them?"

Kaiven didn't need to answer because Sloane shrieked as she spotted her two Valox friends standing beside a Vandar raiding ship, one with black braids and one with wavy, blue hair.

"Thea! Cassie!" She launched herself at the women, enveloping them in a fierce hug then pulling back and meeting her gazes in turn. "I'm so glad you're back!"

"So are we." Cassie rubbed the back of her neck and sighed. "I was afraid I might not even make it onto the escape ship."

Thea frowned. "The Zagrath were hot on our tail, and I thought we'd lost her for a second."

"I think they stunned me or something." Cassie gave herself a small shake. "One of the Zagrath grabbed me, then I felt the buzz of being hit with something, but Thea and Ayden fired at them and got me onboard."

Ayden stepped forward. "That was the easy part. The Zagrath fired on us as we flew away—don't ask me how they could target us—and the ship barely made it back here."

I glanced at the scorched and smoking ship behind him. It looked as bad as it smelled, the acrid scent making my nose twitch. "Were the Zagrath able to track you here?"

"If they did, they did nothing about it. That Zagrath ship is no longer there."

We all turned to the voice that delivered this news. Raas Kaalek approached from behind, his black leather shoulder armor rippling like shiny scales down his arms. My battle chief hadn't mentioned that our Vandar ally had joined us, but I hadn't given him much chance to talk once he'd told me about Ayden's wrecked ship.

"Raas Kaalek arrived just after Ayden," Kaiven said to me under his breath.

"I came to cement our alliance and brotherhood in person." Raas Kaalek clicked his heels together. "I am honored to finally meet the Lost Vandar."

"The honor is ours." I returned the salute with a sharp tap of my heels and all the Vandar around me followed suit. "But we are no longer lost."

"You are not," Kaalek said. "You are a part of the greater Vandar empire. You are one of us."

My chest felt tight as I nodded. Being in the presence of another Raas of the Vandar gave me a sense of belonging that I'd never experienced when my father had talked of the Vandar and my fate in exacting vengeance from them. His bitterness had seeped into all of his memories and made them drip with poison. But casting off my dark mission of revenge had been like throwing off a heavy shroud that had blinded me to the truth. Now that I no longer saw the Vandar through the bitter eyes of my father, the world was a different place. It didn't hurt that I was also completely in love.

I snuck a glance at Sloane, my pulse quickening, before I looked back at my new Vandar brother. "It is our honor to join the Vandar hordes."

"Now, we can do more than secure our alliance," Kaalek continued. "We can band together to eliminate the Zagrath once and for all."

"We need to go after them," Sloane agreed. "If we don't stop them, they'll come back stronger than ever and punish the galaxy for rebelling against them."

Kaalek rocked back on the heels of his black boots. "Your female is correct."

Thea folded her arms over her chest. "She's not his female."

"She was our friend first," Cassie added.

"Don't take it personally," a redhead drawled as she sauntered up behind Raas Kaalek and slapped a hand on his back. "The Vandar think all women who wander near them are theirs."

The Raas lifted a brow at her. "Not true. Only the insolent ones who encroach on our territory and challenge our authority."

"Are there any other types of human females?" Kaiven muttered low so only I could hear him, even though Sloane cut her eyes to him for a beat.

"Don't let my husband's bluster scare you," the woman said, sliding a mischievous glance at the Raas who radiated danger and power. "He's not as ruthless as the stories make him out to be."

"Are you Tara?" Sloane stared at the woman with a messy bun who was dressed in a form-fitting black outfit crisscrossed with studded leather, much like her Vandar mate.

The human grinned and nodded. "You must be Sloane." She glanced at the female with brown skin and braids. "Thea told me all about you."

"Not all," Thea said, giving Sloane a crooked smile. "I didn't tell her about your bizarre taste in old Earth music."

Sloane leveled a gaze at her friend. "Thanks." Then she pivoted to Thea. "And thank you for talking the Vandar into coming to the meet."

"It didn't take much convincing." Tara slipped her hand into Kaalek's. "The Vandar have an alliance with the Valox. Besides, the idea of an unknown Vandar horde was too intriguing to ignore."

"Unknown no longer." Raas Kaalek locked eyes with me, and the hint of a smile teased the corner of his mouth.

"This is great." Sloane rubbed her hands together. "If we're all allies and friends, then we can work together to chase down the Zagrath. They're clearly still a danger to us all."

Raas Kaalek's expression darkened. "Like I said, the imperial ship is gone, but we have tracked where it went."

Thea exchanged a hopeful look with Sloane and Cassie. "Great. Then let's stop wasting time."

"It is not so simple." Kaalek rocked back on his heels. "The Zagrath have retreated to the Jarlevon sector."

"Fuck." Sloane's shoulder sagged while her friend Thea bowed her head.

I did not know what made the sector so fearsome, but I would not back down now. "This Jarvelon sector cannot be more terrifying than our united Vandar hordes."

Raas Kaalek's fierce expression faltered for a beat. "Let's hope not."

My heart thundered in my chest at his words. The danger did not scare me. Not when I would be fighting alongside my brothers. "Then we will fight together—for Vandar."

Kaalek placed a thick hand on my shoulder, his eyes glittering and dark as he nodded. "For Vandar."

EPILOGUE

"Did you do what I asked?" The Zagrath commander did not pivot to face the imperial soldier who entered his ready room. He remained staring out the glass that peered into space.

"We did not capture the resistance fighters, Commander. As requested, we only tagged them. One, to be exact."

The commander gave a curt nod, his lips in a line so tight they'd gone white. Only one. He bit back a snarl and released a breath. One would be enough if he was right. "You're sure you implanted a tracker, and it is activated?"

The soldier clasped his hands behind his back and held his chin high even though the commander didn't look at him. "We are certain. It enabled us to track their ship, even though it was invisible to any other tracking."

The Zagrath commander's lips curled into a cold smile. "Good."

The soldier cleared his throat. "I thought it was crucial that we obtain a member of the Valox resistance. We could have captured her and forced information from her."

The commander spun on his heel. "As enjoyable as it would have been to torture one of those upstart rebels, they would only have come after her bent on revenge."

The soldier thought about the microscopic tracker that had been shot into the back of the female's neck. They were hanging all their battle strategy on *that*? "Now they won't come after us?"

"Oh, they will, but as long as that rebel is with them, we will see them coming." The commander curled his fingers into a fist. "The enemy won't be so unknowable anymore." Then he chuckled, the sound void of any mirth. "They thought they'd destroyed us. As if an empire as vast as ours could be eliminated so easily. They will soon learn how far our power truly stretches."

The soldier looked beyond his commander to the strange purple and green lights cavorting across the blackness of space, punctuated every few moments by a pop of light. He would never question his superior officer's judgment, but the Jarlevon sector seemed like a dangerous gamble. Did the empire really have enough might and influence to control the mercenaries and pirates who occupied this region of space? Only those with a death wish—or a desire to keep their criminal activities hidden—ventured into the Jarlevon sector with its frequent geomagnetic storms and electromagnetic anomalies. Would the Valox resistance and Vandar hordes risk it?

"They will come," the commander said, as if he could hear the soldier's thoughts. "Even if they survive this sector, they will not survive us."

∾

THANK YOU FOR READING PRODIGAL! Turn the page for your bonus epilogue! If you liked this steamy sci-fi romance, you'll love the next book in the series, PRISONER.

What's more dangerous than venturing into the Jarlevon sector to crush the Zagrath? Being stranded with the deadly and ruthless creatures who rule the sector—and consider prisoners to be expendable.

∾

This book has been edited and proofed, but typos are like little gremlins that like to sneak in when we're not looking. If you spot a typo, please report it to: tana@tanastone.com
Thank you!!

BONUS EPILOGUE

Thank you for pre-ordering Prodigal! Here is your bonus epilogue!!

Sloane

"ARE you sure we should be doing this?" I asked, taking a break from humming 'It was the Heat of the Moment' and looking nervously from Cassie to Thea as we stood in the corridor outside the hangar bay. "We do have some imperial ass to kick."

"The Vandar are still working on the best attack plan when we go after the Zagrath." Cassie stepped back and eyed me. "I can't think of anything I'd rather do in the meantime than hold your Raisa ceremony."

I narrowed my gaze at her. "I didn't even think you liked Ronnan after the whole abduction thing."

Thea shrugged as she adjusted my headpiece so that the dark, silken cords weren't hanging in my face. "We've decided to forgive and forget that since he did come save our butts when we were taken captive by the enemy."

"Cheap dates," I muttered, shooting a wicked grin at my friends.

"I think it's romantic," Cassie sighed. "You met under difficult circumstances but love triumphed anyway, and now you're getting married."

I felt like saying that the circumstances were only difficult because Ronnan had insisted on keeping me as his prisoner, but then I decided that Thea's forgive-and-forget policy was probably a good one to have when it came to how I met the Raas.

"Not married," Thea corrected. "This is just the ceremony to make her his Raisa."

"Which is the Vandar equivalent of getting married," I said.

Thea's jaw dropped. "Wait. We're getting you ready for your actual wedding?"

Cassie laughed and shook her head. "Someone's been too busy tinkering with the Vandar technology to pay attention to what's going on."

Thea flipped one of her shiny braids off her shoulder. "I've been paying attention." Her gaze darted to the floor and then back up. "You can't blame me for being fascinated by the Vandar tech. And the Kyrie Vandar have some modifications even the other Vandar have never seen. I would love to visit their home world and check out Selkee technology."

Mention of the Selkees made me think of Ronnan. He'd insisted that he was fine having no family at our ceremony. I knew he would have wanted to have his mother attend, but she was gone. He'd insisted that he didn't need anyone but me, which was sweet, but made me wonder about the Selkee brother and other siblings back on his home world.

"So, let me get this straight." Thea put a hand on one hip as she gave my outfit the once-over. "Vandar females get married in this?"

I looked down at the black, sheer fabric that draped from one shoulder and spilled down my body until it trailed behind me. It was cinched at the waist by narrow, silver chains that criss-crossed under my breasts, and the skirt was slit high on one side.

"I think it's beautiful." Cassie reached for my hand and squeezed it. "You look gorgeous. Fierce and gorgeous."

She was right. Vandar bonding ceremonies in which a Raas took a Raisa didn't have any white fluff or puffy dresses. My Raisa gown made me look like more like a vengeful warrior than a blushing bride. Not that I minded. I liked the idea of being a Raisa and flying with Ronnan and his horde. It was more fitting for a resistance fighter, anyway.

"Do you get to carry your own battle axe?" Thea asked.

"During the ceremony?" I laughed. "Probably not."

"Makes sense." She nodded thoughtfully. "I'll bet a lot of Vandar brides have wanted to kill their mates."

Cassie snorted back a laugh as she flicked a hand through the blue waves that fell across her shoulders. "I've never met a Vandar female. I wonder if they're as scary as the males."

Thea waved a hand at my dress. "At least we know *they* don't go bare breasted."

"I'm impressed the Vandar could whip up a dress," Cassie said. "Since they seem to wear large quantities of leather, I'm a little surprised they had the exact fabric needed to make a ceremonial Raisa dress."

"They didn't." The unfamiliar voice made us all turn at a short, stocky creature with copper-colored skin and richly striped horns that curled around his ears. He was dressed in layers of textured fabrics—nubby, brown pants topped with a burgundy paisley vest glittering with gold buttons. A silky blue shirt puffed up from beneath his vest, the sleeves rolled up nearly to his elbows. "Tara called in a favor for you."

"Are you...?" I remembered Tara mentioning an alien friend who was a skilled tailor, but I'd also thought he lived on Carlogia Prime.

He smiled, and his heavily lined face lit up. "Master Tailor Fenrey at your service."

"Don't you live on Carlogia Prime?" I asked. "Or do you now live on Raas Kaalek's horde ship with Tara?"

Fenrey choked back a laugh. "Wouldn't Kaalek love that?" Then he shook his head. "No. I can't abide by the Vandar warbirds. Too big and echoey for me. I prefer my cozy home and workshop." He began to circle me, eyeing the dress. "Tara sent a ship to bring me here and create your dress. Silly woman thought I'd be able to live with myself without seeing it on you and doing a final fitting."

"Final fitting?" Thea cut her gaze to the hangar bay doors down the corridor. "She's about to walk down the aisle."

Fenrey wrinkled his squat nose. "I don't know if I'd call it an aisle."

I shot Cassie a desperate look. "There's no aisle?"

"There's an aisle." Cassie bobbed her head up and down, as if reassuring herself as much as me. "It's just not your typical wedding aisle. It's more of a circular path."

"Tara told me it mimics the pattern of the Vandar battle axes," Fenrey said absently, as he tucked the fabric near my waist. "Don't be startled when you see all the Vandar warriors lining the way with their axes drawn. It's all part of the ritual."

I gulped. "Ritual?"

"I am so glad the Vandar don't believe in bridesmaids," Thea said under her breath.

Before I could register my growing doubts, Fenrey released a loud breath.

"I must say, I've outdone myself again." He folded his stubby arms across his chest. "It's perfect, my dear."

"Just in time!" Tara rushed toward us. Her red hair was down, the wild mass falling in a torrent of curls down her back, and she wore a black skirt instead of form-fitting pants. Other than that, she still looked like a female version of Vandar raider.

Fenrey spun on one heel. "She's ready."

"I don't know about that." I let out a nervous laugh as my hands trembled. Suddenly, this all seemed very real and a bit scary. "Fenrey mentioned something about a ritual?"

Tara flapped a hand at me as she pulled me toward the hangar bay. "Ceremony, ritual. Same thing."

Cassie hurried along beside me. "But are they?"

When we reached the broad doors that were closed, Tara stopped and turned to face me. "You love Ronnan, right? You want to be with him, right?"

"Yes," I stammered, "but—"

"Then the rest doesn't matter." She gave me a warm smile. "Trust me."

I eyed the human woman who'd been a pilot for the empire before being taken prisoner by Raas Kaalek. I'd heard that they'd started our despising each other. I guess if she could be happy being a Raisa for the Vandar, anyone could.

Tara hurried forward and my friends followed her, with Cassie blowing kisses and Thea giving me a double thumbs-up. The doors swished open for them, revealing a darkened hangar bay, and then closed again.

My pulse spiked. Why was it so dark in there?

"Don't worry, my dear." Fenrey voice from behind made me jump. "I have your train."

I glanced at him standing a few paces back with the hem of my dress in his hands. For some reason, even though I didn't know the alien well at all, I was comforted by his presence and his warm smile.

Then the doors swished open again, and Fenrey gave me a nod to start walking. I took tentative steps over the threshold and into the massive space that usually bustled with clanging and shouts. Now it was almost eerily quiet and dark.

As my eyes adjusted, I could see Vandar raiders holding lit torches along the perimeter of a large circular space. Within that circle, stood more Vandar creating a long arch with their extended arms and clutched axes. The Vandar faced each other in pairs and the blades of their axes touched where they met in the air. Through the enormous warriors, I could see Ronnan waiting for me in the center.

I swallowed down any residual fear and stepped up to the gauntlet of raiders and the axes that were held so that the blades faced down. Fenrey released the train of my gown, and it fluttered to the floor behind me, as he stepped back and vanished into the shadows.

I took another step forward, passing the first pair of Vandar who stood across from each other. As I cleared them, they swung their axes down, and the blades sliced through the air behind me. I stifled a yelp, as I felt a gust of air from the axe swings.

"*Vaes!*" Ronnan bellowed from deep within the labyrinth of Vandar. He'd used that word to beckon me before, but now it sounded more intense, more commanding.

The warriors I'd just passed echoed his call. "*Vaes!*"

A chill went through me, although part of it was tinged with desire. Totally normal, I told myself as I took another step and passed another pair of Vandar. Their axes swung down behind me and Ronnan roared again.

"*Vaes!*"

This time the four warriors I'd passed echoed his command, the sound reverberating around me.

I continued walking, the axes continued swinging, and the bellows of Ronnan and the Vandar grew almost deafening by the time I reached the center of the coiling path of warriors. When I was standing beside Ronnan and the echoes of the roars of every Vandar I'd passed had quieted, I let out a breath.

Raas Kaalek stood in front of us to perform the ceremony. Although his face was stern, I saw a hint of a smile tease his lips. "Now the easy part is over," he said to me in a low voice.

I gaped at him for a beat before I saw that Ronnan was fighting back a smile. I narrowed my gaze at my husband-to-be. "You didn't think I'd scare so easily, did you?"

"Not for a moment," he growled. "Not after you tried to kill me in my own bed."

Now Raas Kaalek was smiling fully, but he cleared his throat and gave us both a serious look. He pivoted slightly to Ronnan.

"Raas Ronnan, do you honor Lokken and the gods of old by taking this woman as your Raisa? Do you entwine your life with hers until you are called to Zedna with the ancients? Do you so swear it?"

Ronnan slid his gaze from Kaalek to me, his dark eyes glinting as they held mine and made my knees go weak. "I swear it."

I agreed to whatever Kaalek asked me, the words a blur to me as I swore my life to Ronnan's. Then he was sweeping me into a hard kiss and lifting me off the ground as the Vandar roared their approval. They pounded the handles of their axes on the floor, and the sound pulsed through me.

Ronnan released me just enough so he could move his mouth to my ear. "It is done," he husked. "You are mine."

"And a Raisa of the Vandar," I whispered back, pulling my head away enough to meet his gaze and jerk my head toward the door with a wicked smile. "*Vaes!*"

ALSO BY TANA STONE

Raider Warlords of the Vandar Series:

POSSESSED (also available in AUDIO)

PLUNDERED (also available in AUDIO)

PILLAGED (also available in AUDIO)

PURSUED (also available in AUDIO)

PUNISHED (also available on AUDIO)

PROVOKED (also available in AUDIO)

PRODIGAL

PRISONER

The Tribute Brides of the Drexian Warriors Series:

TAMED (also available in AUDIO)

SEIZED (also available in AUDIO)

EXPOSED (also available in AUDIO)

RANSOMED (also available in AUDIO)

FORBIDDEN (also available in AUDIO)

BOUND (also available in AUDIO)

JINGLED (A Holiday Novella) (also in AUDIO)

CRAVED (also available in AUDIO)

STOLEN (also available in AUDIO)

SCARRED (also available in AUDIO)

The Barbarians of the Sand Planet Series:

BOUNTY (also available in AUDIO)

CAPTIVE (also available in AUDIO)

TORMENT (also available on AUDIO)

TRIBUTE (also available as AUDIO)

SAVAGE (also available in AUDIO)

CLAIM (also available on AUDIO)

CHERISH: A Holiday Baby Short

PRIZE

Inferno Force of the Drexian Warriors:

IGNITE (also available on AUDIO)

SCORCH (also available on AUDIO)

BURN (also available on AUDIO)

BLAZE

FLAME

COMBUST

THE SKY CLAN OF THE TAORI:

SUBMIT (also available in AUDIO)

STALK

SEDUCE

SUBDUE

STORM

ALIEN ONE-SHOTS:

ROGUE (also available in AUDIO)

VIXIN

All the TANA STONE books available as audiobooks!

INFERNO FORCE OF THE DREXIAN WARRIORS:

IGNITE on AUDIBLE

SCORCH on AUDIBLE

BURN on AUDIBLE

RAIDER WARLORDS OF THE VANDAR:

POSSESSED on AUDIBLE

PLUNDERED on AUDIBLE

PILLAGED on AUDIBLE

PURSUED on AUDIBLE

PUNISHED on AUDIBLE

PROVOKED on AUDIBLE

Alien Academy Series:

ROGUE on AUDIBLE

BARBARIANS OF THE SAND PLANET

BOUNTY on AUDIBLE

CAPTIVE on AUDIBLE

TORMENT on AUDIBLE

TRIBUTE on AUDIBLE

SAVAGE on AUDIBLE

CLAIM on AUDIBLE

TRIBUTE BRIDES OF THE DREXIAN WARRIORS

TAMED on AUDIBLE

SEIZED on AUDIBLE

EXPOSED on AUDIBLE

RANSOMED on AUDIBLE

FORBIDDEN on AUDIBLE

BOUND on AUDIBLE

JINGLED on AUDIBLE

CRAVED on AUDIBLE

STOLEN on AUDIBLE

SCARRED on AUDIBLE

About the Author

Tana Stone is USA Today bestselling sci-fi romance author who loves sexy aliens and independent heroines. Her favorite superhero is Thor (with Aquaman a close second because, well, Jason Momoa), her favorite dessert is key lime pie (okay, fine, *all* pie), and she loves Star Wars and Star Trek equally. She still laments the loss of *Firefly*.

She has one husband, two teenagers, and two neurotic cats. She sometimes wishes she could teleport to a holographic space station like the one in her tribute brides series (or maybe vacation at the oasis with the sand planet barbarians). :-)

She loves hearing from readers! Email her any questions or comments at tana@tanastone.com.

Want to hang out with Tana in her private Facebook group? Join on all the fun at: https://www.facebook.com/groups/tanastonestributes/

facebook.com/tanastoneauthor

instagram.com/tanastoneauthor

amazon.com/Tana-Stone/e/B07V3LRSNH

bookbub.com/authors/tana-stone

tiktok.com/@tanastoneauthor

Made in the USA
Thornton, CO
04/17/23 15:25:21